Mountain Man Daddy Series

Mountain Man Sheriff (Book 1)

S.E. Riley

The Redherring Publishing House

Mountain Man Sheriff (Book 1)

Table of Contents

Prologue

Lauren

I couldn't remember the last time I had been in handcuffs. I was certain that I hadn't been in the back of a sheriff's truck back then, either.

Sheriff Hollis, at least that's what he told me his name was. I have trouble trusting law enforcement these days, especially when he kept looking at me as if I was crazy. I might have screamed if that distrusting look passed across his green eyes one more time.

Fortunately, he didn't look at me again after loading me into the back of the truck. Instead, he was busy running the plates again. I thought he was only running them again to placate me. He didn't seem to believe that my ex-husband would ever tamper with documents to change the ownership of my car.

Maybe this was all karma's way of getting back at me.

I had finally packed my meager amount of things and left my controlling cop husband. When I threw a dart at a map, it landed on Willow Town. This was supposed to be my chance at a new beginning, but instead, I was being driven to the local jail.

What a way to make an impression.

Here I am, Willow Town, newly a criminal and ready to terrorize you all by stealing my own car, I thought as the sheriff drove over the bumpy back roads.

"You know, this is all a mistake. I've already told you that once.

If you would actually listen to me, you might see that I'm telling the truth."

"Miss, you were trying to break into a car on the side of the road. That car back there was reported as stolen. You are either the thief or may have seen something relevant to this case. We can sort that out when we get back to the station."

"Holy shit," I said, leaning back against the seat and trying to adjust my wrists in the cuffs. "You are a real piece of work, aren't you? No wonder you're the sheriff."

"And what's that supposed to mean?" he asked, his jaw clenching as he looked at me in the rearview mirror. "If anyone in this vehicle is a piece of work, it's you. Do you honestly think I would believe that you weren't trying to break into that car? When I pulled up, you were about to throw a rock through the window."

"Because my keys were locked inside *my* car!"

I never would have been arrested if he hadn't pulled up when I tried to break into my own car. I wouldn't have had to do this if the car hadn't broken down in the first place. I had been in a hurry to get out and find out what was wrong with the engine, slamming the door before I remembered to grab the keys.

"You can't prove that. Facts are the car is reported as stolen, and you were going to break a window. While I can't question you on what I think you were about to do, I can question you concerning the stolen vehicle."

"Lucky me," I muttered, closing my eyes, and hoping it would all be over soon.

By the time the questioning was over, the sun had set in Willow Town. I was still without a car as the police tried to figure out what was happening. Apparently, my story of an ex who happened to be a corrupt cop wasn't good enough for them. I had expected as much. Cops never wanted to believe that one of their own could be corrupt—not even if they were from different counties and had never met.

Still, they had pried open the car and given me back the duffel bags that were in the back seat filled with belongings after sifting through them. My car would be held until they determined whether it was mine or not, despite showing them my insurance.

Go figure!

Rather than argue with them, I slung both bags over my shoulders and walked down Main Street. Main Street was one stretch of road that seemed to house the commercial district of Willow Town. Everything you needed was on this one short stretch of town. I tried to find my new workplace and home while looking around at the small buildings. Most of the buildings were quiet, their lights off, and their curtains were drawn. It was too late at night for anyone to be awake unless they were patrons of the one and only bar in town.

When I entered Taz less than 10 minutes later, there was a woman with bright blue hair behind the bar. She looked up at me and smiled, speaking to one of the other bartenders quickly. She rounded the bar and joined me, wiping her hands on her towel.

"How can I help?"

"Hi. I'm Lauren...I'm looking for Kayleigh."

"Ah, yes, Lauren. Pleasure to meet you." She shook my hand firmly before looking at her watch. "Thought you'd be here earlier? Did you get lost on your way here?"

"Sorry, no. Car trouble." I giggled nervously.

"Happens to the best of us," she said, smiling as she reached into the pocket of her apron and withdrew a key. "You must have had a long trip getting here. Go get some rest. The apartment is upstairs. It's small but cozy. If you need anything, come down here and let me know. I'm usually here from noon onwards."

"Thank you," I said, taking the key.

Kayleigh nodded. "I have a bar to tend to. I'll see you tomorrow night at seven for your first shift. Try not to be late."

"Thank you," I said again, turning the key over in my hand. "You don't know how much I appreciate this."

Kayleigh smiled as she walked around the bar. "You sounded like someone who was looking to start their life over. I've been there before."

Smiling, I nodded and backed away from the bar as more patrons clustered around it. "I'll see you tomorrow night."

"Have a good night, Lauren."

I left the bar and headed to the little apartment above it. She was right; the apartment was small, but it was cozy. It was the first place I could call my own since the divorce. Curtains hung over the window, and a few pieces of furniture spread throughout the apartment. It wasn't much, but it was enough to hold me over until I could start buying my own belongings.

Instead of dwelling on what the apartment wasn't, I smiled at what it was. It was the first place I ever had that belonged to me and only me. There was no ex-husband with his name on the lease.

When my head finally hit the pillow later that night, I got the overwhelming sense of finally being home.

Chapter 1

Nate

Saturdays were beer night. Me and my sister Sarah would abandon all our responsibilities and head to Taz for a few rounds. It was a weekly tradition that we had been carrying on for years. I could count the number of times we had missed our beer night on one hand.

Even though I was avoiding the new bartender like the plague—and had been for the last four Saturdays I came in—she wouldn't keep me from beer night.

Arresting her had been the highlight of my month. The entire drive to the station was filled with her incessant chatter about how she couldn't possibly have stolen a car. I didn't believe her at first, or even when we got to the station, but I had been sure she was telling the truth by the time I had released her from custody.

It had taken longer than I would have liked to verify her story, and even then, the story seemed hazy at best. It was only when calling the dealership and giving them the VIN that it was confirmed the car had been sold to Lauren and not her ex-husband. The plates had still been registered to Jason Guthrie, no matter how many times I ran the plates.

Still, there had been something that told me that this woman hadn't stolen the car. There was something about how her eyes had darted around the station, as if looking for her husband, nearly scared that he would pop out of the shadows.

It was too late at that point to make amends. She was pissed off, and there was nothing I could say to make her believe I was just doing my job.

Not that it mattered. Apart from beer nights, Lauren and I hadn't seen each other since then. It was a small town but living on the outskirts—and spending most of my time at the station—helped me avoid majority of the population. It was sometimes lonely, but it was better than watching my ex-best friend walk around with my ex-girlfriend on his arm.

I nursed my beer far in the back corner of the bar, trying to erase the thoughts of my disastrous last relationship from my mind. Despite my efforts to relax and have a good time, there was a brown-eyed blonde that kept skating around the edges of my vision.

Watching her as she worked was something else. Each time I came in on a Saturday, she was working, and she made sure I wasn't in her section. It had been annoying at first, but now, it was entertaining. She was doing everything in her power to ignore me, but I didn't miss how those brown eyes looked at me every now and then.

"Don't hate me for being late," Sarah said as she slid into the chair across from me. "I promise I tried to be on time this week, but my classes were running late, and getting back to town took longer than I thought."

I laughed and shook my head, taking another sip of my beer. "Sarah, relax. School comes first. It's fine."

Sarah grinned as Kayleigh shoved a cold glass of some craft beer in front of her. Kayleigh was gone as quick as she had come, off to serve more of her patrons.

"So," Sarah said, looking over at the bar to where Lauren was determined to ignore us. I caught her eye for a second, winking at her only to see a scowl cross her face. Lauren turned away, smiling at one of the men in front of her.

"So, what?"

"So, you still interested in that bartender?"

I scoffed and shook my head. "I'm not interested in any bartender."

"I forgot that you've sworn off women," Sarah said, smirking around the rim of her glass as she took a sip of her beer.

In a way, she was right. I didn't have time for women in my life and didn't want to have time for them. Not after my last girlfriend had spent most of our relationship cheating on me with my best friend. While I had moved on from that, I still had no interest in dating anytime soon. I was happy alone.

"It's easier this way. I have more time to focus on my career."

Sarah rolled her eyes, leaning on the table. "You do realize that sounds insanely lonely, right?"

"It's fine, Sarah. It's what works for me right now."

She hummed and drummed her fingers on the table, not bothering to say anything more on the subject, easily switching the topic to her classes. As I listened to her talk, I knew that Sarah would make an amazing lawyer one day. She was passionate about helping people and righting wrongs. She loved a good argument. My heart swelled with pride as she talked about some of her lessons.

"Hey," Kayleigh said, approaching the table with a wary smile nearly an hour later. She was carrying two more beers for Sarah and I. "I hate to ask this, but I have to pick up Bryce early on Saturdays from now on. Lauren is still new at closing the bar. Would you mind waiting with her, Nate? Just for the next few Saturdays? I know I shouldn't worry about something happening to her, but it's still late at night with a bunch of drunks lingering."

"Not a problem, Kay. Tell Bryce I say hello," I said before downing the last of my beer.

Sarah waited until Kayleigh had walked away before smirking at me with a knowing look. I said nothing as I sipped at the new, chilled beer. Sarah drummed her fingers on the table, trying to drive me insane. Her smirk grew as I glanced over at the bar, looking for the curvy blonde before looking away.

"We really aren't going to talk about how attracted you are to Lauren?" Sarah asked, her tone light and teasing as she traced her finger through the condensation on her bottle.

"We aren't going to talk about that because you're wrong."

Sarah's smirk drew as she shook her head. "You keep telling yourself that."

"I will."

***

It was well past midnight when Lauren rounded up the last drunks. She helped them outside to waiting cars driven by their wives or loved ones, before heading back inside to clean up. I watched her the entire time from my place at the table in the corner. Though she looked like she was ignoring me, I could tell from the tension in her shoulders that she was aware of my presence.

Instead of acknowledging me, she went to the stereo in the corner and connected her phone. Moments later, some country song was blasting through the bar, and she sang along to it. She raised her hands above her head, twirling around as she worked at cleaning the bar top and drying the glasses. I tried not to watch her, but the way her thick hips swayed was hypnotic.

Lauren worked in silence, acting as if she was the only one in the room, until she moved to the tables at the far end of the room. Every now and then, she would look up at me and scowl before going back to scrubbing away sticky liquids and crumbs of food. Finally, she turned the music down and sighed.

"What?" I asked, smirking as I took a sip of the beer I had been nursing for the last hour.

"You could help clean up," Lauren said, looking at me over her shoulder as she scrubbed at the last of some congealed nacho cheese on a table. "Instead of sitting there and looking pretty."

"You think I'm pretty?" I watched as a red blush crept across her cheeks. She shook her head and moved to another table.

"I don't think about you at all."

"I think you're lying about that," I said, teasing her. "I think you spend more time thinking about me than you ever want to admit. In fact, I'm sure you're thinking about me right now."

"Thinking about murdering you," she muttered, glaring at me over her shoulder.

"You know, you probably shouldn't admit your homicidal tendencies to the sheriff."

The corner of her mouth turned slightly before she again schooled her face into a blank expression. Lauren finished with another table and started cleaning the last. I watched her, wondering what she was thinking about. For years, I had been good at reading people. Not her, though. Never her. Maybe that was part of the interest I had in her. Even though we'd barely exchanged a word over the past month, something about her reeled me in. She kept me on my toes like nobody else ever had.

"Back to my original comment," she said, tossing a rag at me. I caught the rag before it hit my face, grinning at her scowl. "Get off your ass and start cleaning."

"I don't work here," I said, stretching my legs in front of me and crossing them at the ankles. "In fact, I am a paying customer. You wouldn't ask a paying customer to help clean up, would you?"

If looks could kill, I would be dead already. She would have crossed the room and skinned me alive if she had been given half the chance.

She gritted her teeth and shook her head. "You are such a pain in my ass." She grabbed the half-finished bottle from my hand, wiping rather roughly where my beer had been sitting, and walked away.

"Not on purpose," I said, grinning when she turned back to her cleaning.

"I have a hard time believing that your behavior isn't on purpose."

Lauren said nothing else as she finished cleaning the bar. I could have gotten up to help, but that might have given her the idea that I wanted to help her. I didn't. The less fondly she thought about me, the better. If I even stood a fraction of a chance with her, I would ruin it like I ruined every other relationship in my life.

She shone too bright to have her light smothered by my darkness.

When she was finally finished cleaning, I felt like more of an ass than before for not helping her. I didn't apologize as I watched her grab the keys and take off her apron. She hung the apron over a hook behind the bar before moving to the front door.

"You coming or what, Sheriff?"

I got up from the table, smothering the smile that threatened to appear at her irritation. "I don't know. I thought I might stay here a little longer since your customer service skills are outstanding."

"Get off your ass, put up your chair and get to the door or I'll lock you in here and call the police about a robbery."

"Funny," I said, upturning my chair on the table and following her to the door.

Lauren smiled sweetly and shrugged, unbothered that her threats were falling on deaf ears. Instead, she looked amused as she flipped me the middle finger.

"That's mature."

"I never claimed to be mature," she said.

"Well, I wouldn't expect maturity from a criminal such as yourself."

"Watch it, Hollis. You're starting to sound like you're enjoying my company. Wouldn't want that, considering you're an intolerable bastard on your best day."

Instead of getting to know her like I wanted to—goading her into talking to me some more—I stayed silent. I waited with her outside as she locked the door. She kept her mouth set in a thin line as she looked over her shoulder at me before climbing the stairs to her apartment. I waited as one of the few taxis in town idled in the background, the several beers I had adding a haze to my vision.

Still, my mind was clear enough to briefly consider what would happen if I followed her up those stairs.

Chapter 2

Lauren

The sun was beating down, warming the shores of the riverbank. There was something about late summer that made everything seem better. I laughed as Kayleigh balanced Bryce on her hip while wading into the river. The little boy giggled and leaned over her arm, reaching for the shimmering water.

Movement from the other edge of the river caught my eye. When I looked up, I could see Nate standing on the other side, a fishing pole draped over his shoulder and a tacklebox in his hand. He glanced at me for a moment, his mouth setting into a hard line before he picked up the cooler at his feet and walked further down the river.

I watched as he worked methodically, putting a lure on the line before casting it into the water. For a moment, there was a look of peace on his face. That was before he looked up, and our gazes locked. The serene smile was gone and replaced with another deep frown. I rolled my eyes and looked back at my new friend and her son, determined to enjoy the day despite the grouch across the river.

"What's his problem?" I asked, wading into the water with Kayleigh and Bryce. She looked up, scanning the riverbank before her eyes locked on the sheriff of Willow Town.

"Nothing," Kayleigh said, grinning as she set Bryce in the water and held his hand. "He's a good man, but he's a little reserved. Not that I can blame him. He had to grow up fast."

"He always seems irritated with me whenever I see him."

Kayleigh chuckled and shrugged. "That's just his face. He's a grump most of the time, but he's also the kind of man who would give you the shirt off his back if you asked for it."

None of that lined up with the man that I had seen so far. He seemed determined to push my buttons at every turn. He was annoying and irritating. I couldn't stand him, but at the same time, I wanted to get to know him better. I wanted to know what makes him tick. But I would be lying to myself if I didn't feel like wringing his neck and burying him six feet deep every time I saw him.

To say my emotions regarding the sheriff were complicated was an understatement.

"I find that hard to believe," I said, glancing back at Nate. He scowled, turning his back to me.

"Give him time. He'll come around, eventually."

I snorted and ran a hand through my hair as the wind blew. "I don't know about that. He threw me in jail without considering that my story might be the truth. Besides, why would I even want him to come around?"

"To be fair, you did tell me that you were about to break into a car, and your ex is crazy. And you want him to come around because he is hot as hell, and you two have off-the-charts chemistry."

"Yeah, it's not my fau...wait, what? We do not have chemistry," I said, making a point of not looking at the sheriff. "We could not have less chemistry."

Kayleigh rolled her eyes. "Oh yeah? Then why does he show up at the beginning of your shift on Saturday and stay until the end? Or how about how you look like you're going to jump over the bar at him whenever he orders a beer."

"I do not," I said, my voice tight.

"Yes, you do. You look at him like he is the most attractive man you've ever seen. Hell, you look at him like you would drag him into a closet and have your way with him if you could. Try telling me again how that isn't chemistry."

"I don't even know what chemistry is," I said, trying to find another way out of this conversation. "My ex-husband and I were married at nineteen. Stupidly young, I know. And now I'm twenty-eight, and I have no clue if I even had chemistry with him."

"Oh," Kayleigh said, wiggling her eyebrows at me. "So, you're interested in older men now, then?"

"I'm not."

"I would say that you are. Nate is thirty-five. That's older."

"I'm done with this conversation," I said, wishing the ground would open up and swallow me whole.

"You have chemistry with Nate," Kayleigh said, looking over at the sheriff and giving a small wave. "You should see what would happen if you explored that with him."

"Shut up." I grinned, my cheeks flushing a bright red, as I crouched down to splash a little wave at Bryce. The boy squealed and jumped, water splashing everywhere.

For the rest of the morning, we played in the water as I squelched any thoughts of the sheriff. At some point, he packed up his fishing gear and left, giving me one more scowl before waving amicably at Kayleigh and Bryce.

Well, fuck you too. I snarled in my mind as I turned around to splash around the water some more. As noon approached, thoughts of the sheriff were in the distant past as I had easy fun with Kayleigh and her son.

Kayleigh was a good boss, but she was a better friend. There was a part of me that worried about getting close to her. If my ex found out where I was—and I didn't doubt that he already had—it might put Kayleigh and Bryce at risk.

When I left them that afternoon, I was certain that I would do whatever it took to keep them safe. That meant that I would keep Jason away from them at all costs. I'd keep my distance as much as possible, but I wanted a friend. I needed a friend.

By the time I got home, I was done worrying about Kayleigh and Bryce. My ex had always been crazy and controlling, but he had never been dangerous. They would be safe. It was me he was after and nobody else.

At least, I didn't think he was until I saw the picture taped to my front door. It was a picture taken on the day I was married, my white dress hugging my body as my ex-husband stood behind me with his arms wrapped around my waist. In the picture, we looked happy. There was no sign of what was to come.

My heart was hammering in my chest as I tore the picture down and crumpled it up. For a moment, I hesitated outside. I didn't want to enter the apartment in case he was in there. I reached out and tried the handle, breathing a sigh of relief when I found it was still locked.

"He's just messing with your head," I said softly as I unlocked my door. "He's messing with you, but he isn't here. He can't bring you back."

With that in mind, I entered my apartment and got ready for work.

***

The bar was open, but Kayleigh had given me the early shift. It was only midnight, and the party in Taz would remain open for a few more hours, given that it was another Saturday night in Willow Town. I smiled and waved to some of the regulars as I left for the night, eager for the cool night air to hit my skin.

The wind was blowing softly, easing the heat of the day as I walked outside. I tilted my head back and looked up at the stars littering the sky. Back in the city, I was lucky if I was able to see any stars.

As I climbed the stairs to my apartment above the bar, there was an uneasy twist in my stomach. When I turned the corner of the landing and saw the door to my apartment was wide open, my heart froze in my chest. My knuckles turned white as I gripped the railing and climbed a step higher. Shattered glass coated the mat in front of the door, a picture of me and my friends torn in half among the mess.

Without thinking, I turned and ran down the stairs. I took a deep breath before I entered the bar, trying to remain calm as I scanned the room for the man I knew would still be there. When my eyes locked with the sheriff's, I crossed the room to his table.

"I need help," I said before he could say anything else.

Nate set down his drink, his green eyes searching my face. What he was looking for, I didn't know, but whatever he saw had to have been enough. He stood up, towering over me, and nodded to the door.

When we got outside, he stopped and crossed his arms. "What's happening, Lauren?"

"My apartment was broken into. I think it's my ex. A picture from my wedding was taped to the door the other day when I got home, but I didn't think much of it. I thought that he was only messing with me. I didn't think that he would break in."

"Stay down here," he said as we stopped at the bottom of the stairs. "If you hear anything while I'm up there, run to my truck and get in. Make sure the doors are locked behind you, and then call the station."

"We can just wait for the cops to get here. You don't have to go up alone."

He chuckled and rolled his eyes. "I'm fine, Lauren. Just run for the truck if you hear anything strange."

I nodded, looking to where his truck was parked less than ten feet away. He normally parked in one of the spaces by the stairs to my apartment on Saturday nights. Try as he might, pretending he didn't care, a part of me knew he parked there to make sure I was safely in my apartment before he left.

Now, even my apartment didn't seem safe.

"Nate," I said, my voice catching in my throat as he walked

away. "I'm scared. What if he's down here and waiting for me?"

Nate looked at me for a moment, the look in his eyes softening. "Come with me then, but stay behind me. If I tell you to run, you do it without arguing."

"Fine," I said, glaring at him.

Nate took the stairs two at a time, pushing the door open wider with the toe of his boot. I stood behind him, my arms wrapped around my torso as I tried to hold myself together. My heart was hammering in my chest as Nate turned the living room lights on, and I could see the full damage done.

Clothing was scattered across the room, torn in half. Pictures I had kept framed on the walls were thrown to the ground and destroyed. As we walked down the hall to the bedroom, I could see lotion and perfume bottles shattered in the washroom.

If the living room was bad, my bedroom was worse. The sheets were ripped and torn into pieces. Stuffing from my pillows covered the floor. Drawers had been thrown open, and their belongings spilled throughout the room.

"This is a mess," I whispered, my eyes wide as I looked around. There was a sharp pain in my chest as the room seemed to grow impossibly smaller.

Nate crossed his arms and turned around slowly, taking in the room and its destruction. He sighed, glancing at me.

"Are you okay?"

"No."

"I'll deal with this. Just keep trying to hold on, okay?"

I nodded. "Okay."

Nate's arms dropped, and he pulled out his phone. He paced away from me as he dialed a number and waited for the call to connect. Even as he stood a distance away, he kept his eyes trained on me.

My heart was hammering in my chest as he stared at me. I felt as if I was out in the open and vulnerable. It was as if someone was seeing me for the first time and stripping back the protective layers I kept in place to keep myself safe.

After a few more moments, he tucked the phone into his pocket. Time seemed to move fast from then, my mind a blur. Red and blue lights lit up the night soon after, as one of the officers came around the corner. Nate grabbed me by the shoulders and led me downstairs. He walked me over to the car that had just pulled up. Two officers jumped out. Nate went back up with one of them. I stood there, shivering, even though it was a warm night.

"Lauren, what's happening?" Kayleigh asked, though it was difficult for me to acknowledge her presence. I was experiencing the world around me through a foggy lens.

"I don't know," I said. Kayleigh wrapped a blanket around me, squeezing my arms as the officer who had remained with me started getting my statement, asking me questions to which I was giving one-worded responses.

At some point, Nate returned alone. By this time, patrons from Taz had walked out, trying to figure out what was happening.

After giving my statement, I turned to Nate, my mind clearing up a bit. Instinctually, survival mode began to kick in.

"Is there any way we can go and get my wallet? I need it to rent a motel room for the night."

Nate's eyebrows furrowed. "Why don't you stay with Kayleigh for the night?"

"Yes, you can stay..." Kayleigh began to say, but I interrupted her.

"I can't. If my ex does anything to them, I will never stop blaming myself. A motel is fine for the night."

Kayleigh and Nate both sighed.

"You're not staying at a motel. It's not safe. You'll stay at my house for the night, and then we'll figure out what comes next in the morning." I opened my mouth to argue, but he gave a sharp shake of his head before pulling keys from his pocket. "Let's go. These officers will take care of things here."

"Like hell you're driving," I said, trying to grab his keys. Nate moved quickly, holding the keys high above his head. "You've been drinking."

"I had a few beers, Lauren. I'm fine. Well below the legal limit."

I glared at him. "Give me the damn keys, Copper. You, of all people, should be following the law, don't you think?"

"Lauren."

"Nate."

"Now who's the pain in the ass?" he asked, still holding the keys high above my head. "It's fine, and I'm fine, Lauren. You're the one that's not fit to be driving. Not after finding out that your apartment was broken into."

"Don't pretend you care more than you have to. Just give me the damn keys and stop being stubborn."

"Fine. For tonight, you win. Don't think that this is ever going to happen again, though. Nobody drives my truck."

He tossed them to me before stalking toward his truck, leaving me no room for argument. I scowled at his back, considering tossing the keys into the bushes. Tossing the keys would mean that both of us would have to walk to his house. I wasn't sure I wanted to spend that much time with him right now, especially not in the open, in case Jason was watching.

As much as I wanted to piss him off, I needed a place where Jason couldn't reach me for the night. Nate was offering me that place, and I wasn't about to turn him down. Now that the shock was starting to wear off, I realized that there was only one motel in town; if Jason was staying anywhere, it would be there. I couldn't risk it. Nate was the sheriff, and his house was the safest place I could be. Jason wouldn't do anything with Nate around.

Kayleigh chuckled beside me. I had honestly forgotten she was standing beside me.

"What?" I asked her, fingering Nate's keys in my palm.

"Oh, nothing. Seems you are in safe hands, then." She winked as she walked off towards Taz.

My mind was too jumbled up to read the tone in her voice, so

I followed Nate towards his car.

"About time," Nate said as I got behind the wheel.

"Shut up," I muttered, adjusting the seat and mirrors to accommodate my height. "Where am I even going?"

"Old Mill Road. Head toward the edge of town, and when you see a dirt road, get on it."

"Fantastic."

"You're more than welcome to walk," he said, his tone gruff as he crossed his arms, tilted his head back, and closed his eyes.

"How am I supposed to know where I'm going if you're taking a damn nap?" I asked, as the truck rumbled to life with a twist of the key.

"End of Old Mill Road is another road. Turn left. My house is at the end."

"Great company," I muttered, following his directions.

The corner of his mouth turned slightly, but he said nothing, continuing to sit with his eyes closed.

The drive to his house was bumpy and isolated. Nate's soft snores filled the truck. When I pulled up outside his house, my mouth nearly dropped open. Everything was dark stone, warm-toned wood, and glass. It was modern but set far away from the rest of town. Isolated.

I turned off the engine and stared at the house. "This is where you live?"

"Apparently," Nate said, opening his eyes before getting out of the truck. "It's where you'll be staying tonight, too. Now, hurry up. My night was ruined, and I would like to get some sleep before I have to work tomorrow."

"Ass," I muttered under my breath, following him to the house and wondering how I would survive a night with him.

Chapter 3

Nate

When I woke up to singing in the morning and the sound of a shower running, my first instinct was to grab my gun. The second was to hop in a cold shower of my own and forget who was naked down the hall. The cold shower would shock me out of imagining what would happen if I walked down that hallway and joined her, running my hands up and down her curves.

If I got in the shower with her, that would be the end of the careful boundaries we had drawn between us. The attraction that had been simmering would boil over.

If I let her in, I wouldn't be able to let her go.

Bringing Lauren here had been a bad idea. There were dozens of other places I could have sent her for the night, but instead, I brought her here. The only person besides myself who had ever been here was my sister. That was the way I wanted it. I didn't want people in my space. I wanted to be alone, but I had brought Lauren here. I had taken the first step in letting her into my life. It scared the living hell out of me.

What the hell am I doing?

I got out of bed and ran a hand down my face, wondering what I was supposed to do now. It was clear that Lauren was already awake, and I wouldn't have any time to think about the next step. She would be on my ass about something the second she knew I wasn't sleeping. Honestly, I was amazed that she hadn't woken me up just so she could be on my ass about something.

When my phone started ringing, I was grateful for a few more seconds of delay.

"Hello, Sheriff."

"Lawson, what's the news on the apartment?" I asked, not bothering with the pleasantries.

"Unsure of who was in here, but it seemed too personal to be a stranger. Too targeted. More likely, it was somebody close to her. We've lifted some fingerprints from the scene, but it was only one set, and we suspect they're Lauren Guthrie's."

"Alright, I'll be there shortly to look at the state of things with fresh eyes. Seal the apartment until I get there, and keep an officer stationed by the door."

"Yes, sir."

As soon as the call ended, Lauren came barging into the room. Her wet blonde hair hang down her back in loose waves. She crossed her arms over her ample chest and stood in the doorway like she owned the place. It bothered me. Lauren was too comfortable in my space. I didn't want her to be comfortable. I wanted her to go home and forget that she had ever been brought over here.

Still, I wasn't letting her see that her being in my private space set me on edge. I didn't want her to think that she had the upper hand in any situation. If she was going to invade my space, I wouldn't let it bother me.

"What the hell are you doing?" I asked, standing up and stretching. "This is my room, in case you missed the closed door."

"Didn't miss it, just ignored it." Lauren perched herself on the edge of my dresser. Her long tan legs stretched in front of her as her shorts rode up. She fidgeted with the buttons of her sleeveless blouse, picking at a stray thread.

I looked away, trying not to stare at her. After a few moments, I looked back at her legs, wondering what they would feel like wrapped around my waist. She smirked at me as if she could read my mind. Scowling, I stared at her, daring her to look away. Lauren met my glare with a look of amusement, fire dancing in her eyes. Playing with her was a dangerous game.

"What do you want?" I asked.

"I heard you on the phone."

I cocked an eyebrow at her and crossed my arms. She had to be the most annoying person I had ever met, but that didn't seem to bother her at all. Instead, she kept inserting herself where she didn't belong. Like behind a door listening to private phone calls.

Lauren looked like she was making herself more comfortable as she leaned back against the mirror and propped one foot on the dresser's edge. I wanted to haul her off the dresser and toss her on the bed. However, that wouldn't improve the situation between us.

"And?"

She rolled her pretty brown eyes. "Are we going back to my apartment or what?"

"A normal person would say thank you."

I sighed and ran a hand through my hair. I tried to think of what else I could do with her. Taking her back to her apartment wasn't safe. Leaving her at the only motel in Willow Town alone wasn't safe either. The best way to watch her and make sure her ex-husband stayed away was to keep her at my place.

"Until we have this entire mess figured out, you can stay here. It's a big house with a good security system."

"That won't cause any gossip around town at all," she said, shaking her head. "Not even a little bit. There is no way that Sally down at the beauty parlor would ever start spreading rumors about how the new girl in town broke into her own apartment just to get that attractive sheriff closer to her."

"And once again, we are back to the fact that you think I'm pretty," I said, smirking as she rolled her eyes.

"I'm just telling you what the elderly women of Willow Town think. Personally, your advanced age is more of a deterrent."

I almost would have believed her if I didn't see the lingering glances she was giving me. "You don't seem to mind my advanced age at all. Thirty-five isn't that old."

"You keep telling yourself that, Grandpa. As if we weren't giving the town enough to talk about. Now they are going to talk about how the elderly sheriff is keeping that nice young woman trapped with him."

"Jesus, Lauren," I said, my voice nearly a growl as I shook my head. "Can't you just say thank you and be done with it like a normal person?"

"I was getting there," she said, a pink flush appearing on her cheeks, but the amused smile didn't fall from her face. "Thank you."

"Get out so I can get dressed."

She smirked and crossed her arms, her eyes trailing over me slowly. I hated the way my body reacted to her stare. Before she could notice the way I was straining against my pajama pants, I disappeared into my closet.

"Get the hell out."

Lauren's laugh filled the room before I heard the door close behind her.

I'm fucked, I thought as I got dressed quickly. The sooner I got rid of her, the better.

***

Not long after I dropped Lauren off at her apartment—making sure that there was an officer there with her—I was called away on a wellness check. By the time I finished with that call, it had been an hour and a half. The entire hour and a half was a war between doing my job and wanting to return to her place to investigate for myself. My officers were good, but I needed to see what we were dealing with. I needed to know how far this ex-husband was willing to go to get her back.

If he wanted her half as much as I did, he was willing to do whatever it took. That was the scary part. I was a rational human being with boundaries. He clearly was not. He had already proven that he was willing to cross lines to be in her life with the fake car theft report, and now this?

I couldn't allow that to happen. He was a threat to her. She had run away from him and their lives together.

My phone started ringing as I left the wellness check, an unknown number flashing across the screen.

"Hello?"

"Well, hello there, Hollis," Lauren said, irritation clear in her voice. "When you brought me here, I told you that I would be packing my bags and driving back to your place to drop them off before coming back to work...though I still think living with you isn't a good idea, but oh well." I drew in a slow breath in response to the tone in her voice. God, this woman was infuriating. "Now, Officer Lawson and I are standing out at my car, and it seems as if the battery has been removed and several cables have been ripped out."

"Stay there with Lawson until I get there," I said, jogging back to my truck, and getting in. I slammed the door shut and cranked the key in the ignition.

Before she could respond, I hung up and tucked the phone back into my pocket. I flicked the sirens on, red and blue lights flashing as I took off down the road. The faster I got to Lauren, the better.

When I got back to her apartment, she was leaning against her car with her arms crossed. Her glare could make weaker men run and hide. I stalked across the parking lot to stop in front of her, matching her glare with one of my own. She tilted her chin upward, daring me to speak.

"Well, I guess you're happy now that I have no choice but to depend on you," she said cooly. The accusation in her voice took me aback. I gritted my teeth, taking a moment to breathe before I said something I would regret. When I was sure I was calm, I closed the distance between us, our bodies nearly pressing against each other. Lauren swallowed hard, but the challenging look didn't vanish from her face.

"Let's get one thing straight..." I said, my tone low as I leaned closer to her, "...I am not a controlling bastard, and I never have been. If you ever accuse me of anything like that again, you'll see what I'm really like."

"Is that a threat?" she asked, the corner of her mouth tipping upward and amusement sparking in her eyes.

I saw red, my hands clenching into fists at my sides. She was in danger, and the only thing that seemed to matter was picking a fight with me?

"Lauren, I'm trying to help. You need to stop acting like you know exactly what is happening and let me do my job as the sheriff of this town."

"Oh?" The smile dropped from her face as she crossed her arms. "I don't know what's happening here. Why don't you enlighten me, Sheriff? It seems like the life I thought I was escaping followed me here."

She scoffed and brushed by me, her shoulder hitting my arm just above my elbow. I took a deep breath, trying not to say something I would regret. Lauren was infuriating—so infuriating that I had a hard time imagining she had ever let her ex push her around.

I headed straight for the car and took over from Lawson, assessing the damage. Minutes later, Lauren stood by my side. I didn't tell her to step back. Lauren bit her bottom lip, watching as I took picture after picture and emailed myself my notes. From what I had seen, she liked to pretend that she was alright when she was really freaking out inside. She was terrified that her ex-husband was getting closer to her, and there was nothing I could do to ease her fear.

At that moment, I had never felt more like a failure at my job.

If looking over my shoulder while I worked would make her feel even a little bit better, I would let her.

"You won't be driving anywhere anytime soon," I said.

"I will drive wherever I want."

"No, you will not. You think that detaching the battery is the worst thing your ex-husband did to your car? Lauren, we need to get Mike, the mechanic, over here to haul your car into the shop and look over it."

"That doesn't mean I'm not going to stay locked up in your house."

"It would be safer than going all over town by yourself and not knowing where he is."

She rolled her eyes and leaned back against the side of her car. "He's a cop. He's not stupid. He won't try to pull anything in the middle of town."

"You don't know that," I said, sending a quick text to the town's mechanic. "You don't know what he's going to do if he sees you alone."

"That's my risk to take," she said, her tone sharp as she walked away from me. "Besides, according to you, I'm a criminal anyway. But don't worry too much about me. I can, and will, handle myself."

She took off before I could say anything else, heading into the bar. I considered following after her but causing a scene in the bar would only result in Kayleigh kicking my ass.

With a sigh, I grabbed the packed bags she had left on the ground and tossed them into my truck. I would pick her up later tonight after she was done working. After that, I would start ignoring her and hope it would make living together more tolerable.

Chapter 4

Lauren

When I stepped outside, Nate was sitting on the front porch, staring out at the trees lining his property. I smoothed down my backless dress and kept my head high, not bothering to look at him as I made my way to Kayleigh's car. It had been a long few weeks, and I needed a break from the man I was sharing a home with.

"You look hot," Kayleigh said as she got out of her car to pull me into a tight hug. "Are you ready to drink until the sun comes up?"

I laughed and nodded, stepping back from her hug to eye her gold dress. "You look amazing too."

"Let's go."

A loud slam of a door sounded behind us. I looked over my shoulder to find the porch empty. With a roll of my eyes, I got into Kayleigh's car and leaned back in the seat.

"What was that about?"

I sighed and ran a hand through my hair, loosening the curls that cascaded down my back. "I'd really rather not talk about it until I've got a few drinks in me."

"That can be arranged."

I grinned as she turned the car around and headed away from Nate's house. With every mile she drove, I could feel the weight lifting from my shoulders. The further away I got, the more the tension melted away.

***

At some point during the night, pitchers of beer turned into shots. We had gone a town over to escape spending time with anyone we knew. Actually, it had been at my request. I didn't want the nosy townspeople to overhear anything we said and gossip about it over coffee tomorrow morning. Sarah was the only exception to the rule. Since I began staying with Nate, Sarah had made a point of coming over every few nights to cook dinner and irritate her brother.

When Sarah walked through the door shortly after we started drinking, I invited her to our table while the waitress brought another empty glass for the pitcher of beer.

"So..." Kayleigh said, pouring herself another glass of beer, "...what is going on with you and the sheriff?"

"Please gloss over all the dirtiest details," Sarah said, sipping her beer. "I don't want to know what you and my brother are doing in his house, but I also kind of want to know. It's been a long time since he let a woman in."

I groaned and threw back another shot, twirling the glass on the table as I considered how much to tell her. Kayleigh had known the sheriff her entire life, and Sarah was his sister. They would see Nate from a different angle than I did.

Still, if we were going to get into the dirty details, she needed to know how I had even appeared on the sheriff's radar in the first place. I suspected that Sarah already knew some of the details, but another part of me said she didn't know anything. Nate didn't seem like the type to tell other people my personal business.

"I know," Kayleigh said, grinning at Sarah. "The chemistry the pair of them have is off the charts."

"I've seen it. Nate didn't look at his ex-girlfriends like that. Ever. He didn't have many while we were growing up—he was too busy taking care of everyone else. But now that he's met her, it's

29

like watching him fall hard and fast for the first time in his life."

"You two are ridiculous," I said, rolling my eyes and finishing my beer before pouring another. I would need more than a couple of drinks to get through my story. "Absolutely insane. There is nothing between us."

"Keep telling yourself that," Sarah said, smirking as she crossed one leg over the other. "Now, start telling us about how you and my brother first fell in love."

I rolled my eyes again, knowing better than to try to argue with her. After spending only a few days with Sarah, it was clear that when she made up her mind about something, she wouldn't change it unless absolutely necessary.

"I left my ex the day I finally had enough money. He had always been controlling, and I was never what he thought the wife of a police officer should be. It was just toxic. The love I thought we had sizzled away quickly, replaced by..." I shuddered, remembering the lonely nights and equally terrifying days. "I got tired of being told what to do and how I should look, so I filed for divorce. Days before I moved to town, my divorce was finalized. The last time I saw Jason in the lawyer's office, he said he would never let me go."

"So, why did he sign the papers?" Sarah asked.

"I never thought he would. I just thought that the papers would stall him long enough for me to escape. Complaining to his boss never worked. Neither did calling other stations and trying to get other officers involved. The police are all for protecting their own and would call Jason. They told him what I was doing."

"If reporting him wasn't working, why would he ever bother signing the papers?" Kayleigh asked, leaning forward on the table.

"I caught him on a phone call one night. He didn't know I was there. He thought that I was out with one of the few friends he approved of. I came home early, though. As soon as I heard him talking about drugs going missing from an evidence locker, I started recording out my phone. I don't know why I recorded it, but call it instinct or whatever. But let's just say I had overheard some conversations like that in the past, and I knew this was my chance."

"What did you get?"

"Enough to convince him that I would go to the district attorney and ruin his career. He was on a burner phone talking to one of the officers he was working with. They were talking about when to steal the drugs and how they would resell them."

"And that's how you were able to force him to sign the paperwork?" Kayleigh said, her eyes widening as a small smile crossed her face. "I always knew you were a badass."

"Reporting him wasn't enough. Blackmail had to be."

"Do you still have copies of those recordings?" Sarah asked.

I nodded, taking a long sip of my drink. "Yes. I wasn't going to give him my only copy, and he knows it. I've got several stored in different places. That was what was keeping him from coming after me immediately."

"What changed?"

"The district attorney started looking around at some other cases. There was an article about it online a few weeks ago. A gun in an important cartel case went missing. Jason was one of the officers who made the initial arrest. Though they haven't said as much, they are likely investigating him as well as the other arresting officers. If he has me back, he has all the other recordings."

Kayleigh draped one leg over the other, leaning back in her chair. "Is that why the apartment was trashed?"

I nodded and swallowed hard as a lump rose in my throat. "Yeah. That was Jason. Maybe he was looking for physical copies of the recordings." I scoffed. "He needs to try harder if it was him. At least, we're pretty sure it was him. Nate has me staying at his place until they find Jason."

"And how's that been going?"

"Well," I said, setting the shot glass down on the table. "The door slamming is a daily occurrence. Plus, he doesn't speak much to me."

Kayleigh smirked and took a sip of her beer. "You sound almost sad about that."

"Shut up. I do not." I grinned and shook my head, pouring my own glass of beer and finishing off the pitcher. "It makes living with him a lot easier. We come and go, and neither of us really has anything to do with each other."

Sarah laughed. "Except the nights I come over. Those nights, the sexual tension fills the room. They both glare at each other like they're three seconds away from ripping each other's clothes off."

"We do not," I said, my cheeks turning a dark red. "I told you before. Nothing is going on between me and your brother."

"I think you should stop lying to yourself," Sarah said, her tone light and teasing as she smirked at me. "Nate has let you in more than anyone else. He's letting you see his world. Hell, he talks about you when you're out of the room and makes you sound as if you are too good to be true."

"I don't think I believe that," I said, my cheeks feeling as if they were an inferno that couldn't be controlled. "He barely even talks to me."

"Because he's emotionally stunted," Sarah said, laughing and shaking her head. "I love him, but it's true."

Kayleigh shook her head. "He's always been a stubborn one. No more worrying about it—and don't argue and say that you're not because I know you are—we are going to drink and have some fun."

As the bartenders cranked the music louder, I downed my beer with a smile. Kayleigh got up to dance, her hands above her head as she moved with the beat. Another round of shots appeared on the table in front of us. I drank both of them before she had a chance, the alcohol flowing through my veins. Sarah laughed and ordered another round, getting up to join us.

"Shouldn't you slow down a little?" Kayleigh asked, eyeing the shot glasses in front of me.

"I haven't had a night like this to relax in years. I want to just forget about my ex-husband and the sheriff and just have fun."

"You know, Nate could be good for you. I think you're good for him," Sarah said as she grabbed my hand and spun me around in a circle.

I laughed and shook my head. "I'm better off alone. Besides, the sheriff can't stand me. He's made that pretty clear."

Kayleigh rolled her eyes. "If you say so."

"I do. Now, come on, I love this song," I said, grabbing Kayleigh by the hand and dragging her onto the dance floor. Sarah was close behind us, singing along with the music as she lost herself to the beat.

We danced and drank until I couldn't feel my legs anymore. I was laughing and having fun, the stress from the last few weeks melting away. It wasn't often that Kayleigh and I had the night off together, so I was going to make sure that I made the most of tonight.

The annoyingly attractive sheriff was far from my mind.

***

The ground seemed a thousand miles away as I danced on top of the table. I stopped counting how many drinks I had once the room became hazy. However, the haze was starting to clear, and I was still dancing. Kayleigh was grinning up at me from where she danced beside the table, her phone in hand.

"Did you take a video?" I asked her, smiling as I twirled in a tight circle.

"Yes, and I sent it to someone who might find it very interesting. He should be walking in any moment now."

Kayleigh smirked as I kept dancing, not entirely registering what she had just said. I moved my hips to the beat, feeling like I was back in college and having the time of my life with my friends.

There wasn't a worry in the world that could touch me. I had been waiting for the better part of nine years to be this free. Now, I finally was.

Kayleigh and Sarah had both stopped drinking a while ago, trying to tell me that it was getting late and that we should slow down. Their words had been lost on me as I let myself go. Everything that had been keeping me chained up for years was gone.

I was going to have a fun night if it was the last thing I did.

Nobody was going to ruin that for me. Never again.

"What do you think you're doing?" a deep voice boomed over the music.

I turned around, the smile dropping from my face, when I saw Nate standing there with a deep frown on his face. He bent down to pick up my heels from where they had landed on the floor. The heels dangled from his finger as he looked up at me.

"Hello, Sheriff," I said with a smirk. The song changed as I continued dancing, turning my back on him. He wasn't going to ruin my fun. I wasn't going to let him.

"I haven't been able to get her down," Kayleigh said, pointing at me.

"Traitor," I said, glaring at Kayleigh before I started giggling. "I can't believe you called him. I was having fun. He's no fun. He's going to make me have no fun too."

"Hold these," Nate said, handing Sarah my shoes. She took them as Nate crossed back into my field of vision. I scowled at him, dancing and refusing to let his presence bother me.

In seconds, his big hands wrapped around my waist, his fingers skimming against my bare back as he lifted me down. I froze for a moment before kicking him in the stomach.

"Hell, Lauren," he said, grunting as he put me on the ground. "Can you act like a damn adult and go get into the truck?"

"I'm having fun," I said, crossing my arms over my chest and quirking an eyebrow. "You go home. I'll be home later."

Nate sighed, moving too fast for me to stop him. One moment I was on the ground, and the next, I was slung over his shoulder with his arm wrapped around my bare thighs. I could feel his fingers on my bare skin, setting off a fire inside me. His fingers dug into my thigh, his grip on my body tight.

"Here are her shoes, Nate. Lauren, you sleep well, yeah. See you tomorrow," Sarah said from somewhere to my left.

"Don't think they'll be doing much sleeping tonight," Kayleigh remarked before the two women started chuckling.

I didn't have it in me to reply. In my stupor, all I did was grin and start humming, swaying slightly as Nate carried me out of the bar.

While sober me was perfectly capable of trying to ignore the attraction I felt for the sheriff, drunk me wasn't. I put my hands on his lower back, lifting myself up enough to stare at his ass.

"You have a nice ass," I said, reaching down to smack it lightly.

Nate froze, his shoulders tensing. "Don't do that again."

I laughed. "Why not, Sheriff?"

"Lauren."

"Sheriff," I mimicked, reaching down to smack his ass again. "Very nice ass."

Nate started walking again, not bothering to respond until he was standing beside his truck. He opened the door and tossed my heels onto the back seat before dropping me onto the seat. I brushed my hair out of my eyes to see the frown set even deeper on his face.

"Why are you upset?" I asked.

"What was that in there?" Nate asked, his tone sharp.

I didn't want to listen to any of his yelling. Not tonight. Tonight was supposed to be fun. Tonight was supposed to be about forgetting all the stress. I didn't want to listen to him yell. I didn't want to fight again.

Maybe that was why I wrapped my legs around his hips and pulled him to me. Before he could react, I was leaning forward and kissing him. His arms bracketed me on either side, one hand coming up to grab my hip. Nate's mouth moved against mine, but when I ran the tip of my tongue along his lower lip, he gave a low groan sending heat straight to my core. Nate pushed his hips against me, his hardened cock rubbing against me through the layers of clothing that needed to go. It was as if he could read my mind, his hands pulling down the straps to my dress, my breasts plopped out. His large calloused hands were on them, squeezing. I moaned, tilting my head back, and his mouth landed on my neck.

Nate's hands tweaked my hard nipples as need ran wild through me. My fingers laced through his hair, pulling him closer while his hands traveled back down my body to lift one of my legs and hook it around his hip.

I moaned, my hands sliding down his body. I flicked open the button of his jeans, my hand sliding inside the waistband to grip his shaft. In that instant, it was as if a bucket of ice-cold water had been poured over his head.

Nate ripped himself away from me, putting feet of distance between us. I could feel the imprint of his fingers on my body, even as he stood there looking like he had received the shock of his life.

I knew what he would say before the words ever left his mouth. It still didn't stop the aching in my heart when he shook his head. Before he could start speaking, I was already mentally building the walls back up around my heart.

"That was a bad idea. You're drunk."

"I knew what I was doing," I said, pulling up the straps of my dress. I may have been drinking, but I knew what I was doing. I had wanted to kiss him, and take me right there. I wanted to lose myself in him.

I was building the wall back up around my heart to keep that from happening.

"Fine, that was a bad idea because it was a bad idea. Is that good enough for you?"

He didn't wait for a response before storming around the front of the truck and getting in. I reached up and wiped away a tear before twisting to face the front and closing the door.

"That can never happen again," Nate said, starting the truck and turning in the direction of Willow Town.

Why does he have to sound like that kiss was the worst thing to ever happen to him?

"Got it," I said, wiping away another tear before willing myself not to cry.

He wouldn't get the best of me.

I wouldn't let him.

This kiss had been a mistake, and I wasn't going to make the same one twice.

Chapter 5

Nate

Tossing and turning all night had done nothing but frustrate me more than I already was when we got home. I replayed the kiss a thousand times in my mind, wondering what would have happened if I had given in. If I had let her grab my hard length. It would have been so easy to lean back in, kiss her senseless and consume all of her. I should have allowed the single thread I was holding onto to snap. I should have kissed her until we both forgot our own names.

Would that kiss have gone further than it already did?

Would I be waking up this morning with her in my bed?

It had been a long time since I had allowed a woman to get anywhere close to me. I kept the few women in my life at a distance, ensuring mutually destructive relationships. For a long time since my last relationship, there had been too much going on in my life to let anyone in.

Yet, Lauren seemed to have a way of wiggling herself beneath my skin and staying there. She wouldn't take no for an answer, and she didn't let me get away with any of my shit.

I shouldn't have pulled away from her last night. I should have kissed her deeper before the hurt look had ever appeared on her face. There were a thousand different things that I could have and should have done.

Instead, I told her that it was a mistake that could never

happen again.

I'm an idiot.

I would be amazed if she ever forgave me for what happened last night. I wouldn't if I were in her position. I would hold on to that anger and allow it to drive me further away until there was a safe distance between us.

If I were her, I would allow a single kiss to ruin everything we had.

When I walked onto the back deck with coffee in hand, I was surprised to see Lauren already awake and sitting in one of the giant chairs. She stared out at the lake with a steaming cup of coffee. She had never been a morning person—at least not as long as I had known her.

For a few minutes, I stood back and watched her. She seemed content to stare at the wilderness before her. It was one of the reasons I had purchased this land and built a house on it. The isolation was a welcome comfort. It was peaceful and quiet in a way that town never was.

I wondered what she saw when she looked out at the forest surrounding the area. Did she see the same sense of lonely isolation that my sister did whenever she visited? Or was Lauren more like me? Did she look out at the woods and find a sense of peace that had been missing until that point?

Her blonde hair was piled on top of her head, and her long legs were draped over the arm of the chair. Lauren was beautiful. There was no doubt about that. She was smart and kind and nothing like the person I had thought she was when she first moved to Willow Town.

I had seen all the differences in who she was, and what I had thought within the few weeks I had been watching her interact with the community around her. It was interesting to watch her walk into a new place and make friends with the people there. She did it with an ease that I would never understand. Out of all the people who lived in town, I was the only one who seemed to have a problem with her in the course of knowing her.

I didn't have a problem with her anymore. At least, no problem other than picturing her naked multiple times a day.

"Morning," she said without looking up from whatever it was she was staring at. "You going to sit down and drink your coffee, or are you going to keep staring at me?"

Warmth flooded my face as I took the seat beside her and sipped my coffee. Was I that obvious? Apparently, I was.

"Do you want to talk about what happened last night?" I asked, my tone unsure. I wasn't in the habit of talking about emotions. It made me wildly uncomfortable, but something about her had me stepping out onto a ledge for her.

"Not even a little bit," she said, sipping her coffee. "It happened. I kissed you. You turned me down. It's fine. I'm an adult, and I can handle rejection."

I wanted to tell her that she was wrong, but she wasn't. I rejected her last night and wasn't prepared to explain why. I ruin everything that I touch. Why admit that to her? It would only send her running in the opposite direction faster than she already was. Trying to deny what she said would only do more harm than good.

"So, did you, Kayleigh, and Sarah have a good time? I didn't really think you were the type to go out and drink your problems away." I winced and took another sip of my coffee. "That wasn't supposed to sound as judgmental as it did."

"Glad you cleared that up," she said, her tone flat as she looked at me for the first time that morning. Her eyes were rimmed with red and dark bags circled beneath them.

"Why were you crying?"

"None of your business, quite honestly."

"Fair," I said, ignoring the small stab of pain in my chest. Guilt washed over me in waves. She had been crying, and no matter what she said, I was sure it had to do with me.

"I'm just worried about Jason and whatever happens next. He

was always controlling, but now he's scary. The mechanic called me. Finally got around to looking at my car even though it's been weeks."

"Small town mechanics aren't known for their speed. What did he say?"

"Brake lines were cut."

My hand clenched around my cup. "I didn't know that. I haven't talked to the mechanic yet."

"Well, now you know. You were right."

"I don't take any pleasure in being right about that. Tell me more about this ex-husband. Jason."

She shook her head. "We got married right after high school. For a few years, we were happy. And then the promotions started, and suddenly I had to change. I had to be like the other officers' wives. He liked to control where I went, what I ate, and how I dressed. Everything. Nine years of my life were spent being his doll. Finally, I saved up enough of my own money and filed for divorce."

"Would that be enough to send him after you like this?"

"Absolutely," she said without taking a moment to think about it. "Appearances are everything to him. His wife walking away from their nine-year marriage would embarrass him. He would do anything to maintain his image, especially when I blackmailed him into signing the papers. If that ever got out, there would be more trouble."

My eyebrows shot upwards. "You blackmailed him?" There was something that I wasn't understanding. She didn't seem like the kind of person who would blackmail others into doing what she wanted, but then again, I don't know her as well as I like to pretend I do. "I'm going to need an explanation, Lauren."

"There was nothing else I could do. I found out about something he had done that would put him in jail for years. I recorded it, blackmailed him, and saved my life. He no longer controls me."

41

"Then why is he coming back around?"

"Did you read the story about the district attorney investigating Crawford City Police for evidence that went missing from a cartel case?" she asked, not looking at me as she spoke.

"Yes."

"He was one of the arresting officers. The district attorney is launching an investigation into the missing gun. It's possible Jason did it. It wouldn't be the first time that he stole evidence and sold it."

"Is that what blackmail you have?" I asked, trying hard to see the situation from her eyes. She was desperate to get out of a controlling marriage. If she had blackmail material, she would and should use it. If I were in her position, I would have done anything I could to escape.

"I have him admitting to stealing and selling drugs. Several copies of it. While he wants me back, he also wants those recordings under his control. Especially now that they're investigating the cartel case."

I nodded and looked down at my coffee. It was a lot to process, and it made Jason incredibly dangerous. "I don't think you should be going anywhere alone until my teams finds him and figures out what to do with him."

She scoffed and shook her head. "No. I'm not hiding from him and his childish games. It isn't happening. I have a life to live, and I'm not going to back down and cower. If he goes down for being a corrupt cop, that's not my problem."

"Lauren, you aren't thinking about this rationally."

She stood up and looked down at me, fire burning in those big brown eyes. "Let me be clear about one thing, Sheriff."

I winced at the way she said sheriff. It wasn't the same playful and teasing tone that she normally used. It was bitter and filled with poison. I wanted her to go back to the playful Lauren, who spent her days lurking around my hallways. I missed the playful Lauren that climbed into my truck every night after work and teased me about the stick up my ass.

"I will not allow you or anyone else to tell me what to do with my life. I lived that way once, and it will never happen again."

"You don't know what you're risking," I said, setting my coffee to the side and standing up. "You have to think about this, Lauren. You need somebody with you. He's less likely to do something if you have someone else with you."

"And I told you!" She stormed closer to me, her chest inches from mine as she tilted her head back to glare at me. "I will not be held under his control again! Not anymore!"

"Lauren!"

"No! Do you hear me? No!"

"I'm not going to let you risk getting hurt," I said, wanting to reach up and run my thumb along her cheek. I had a feeling it would result in coffee being poured all over me.

"Why do you even give a shit?" she asked, her tone sharp as she crossed her arms. "Why now? You didn't give a shit when I told you that my ex-husband was framing me with the car."

I had no good answer. I could tell her I was just doing my job, but that only felt like half the truth. I would have found her somewhere else to stay if I was just doing my job. I would have found her a place that wasn't my own, and I would have only checked in with her when there were updates on the case. It's what I would have done in any other situation.

Instead, I kept the curvy blonde close because I was selfish and stupid. She could protect herself. She didn't need me.

"See?" she said with a nod when I was quiet for too long. "This is exactly what I thought."

"Lauren."

"No. Don't Lauren me. I'm going back to my apartment. It's been weeks without anything happening, and even Jason can't wait around this long. He has a job."

"At least let me drive you back."

She shook her head, her eyes glistening. "I'll call Kayleigh."

"Lauren."

Lauren didn't bother to turn around as she raced into the house and slammed the door shut behind her.

"Shit!" I ran my hands through my hair and looked toward the house. There was no world in which I hadn't made this entire situation worse than it already was.

Chapter 6

Lauren

Three weeks was a long time to deal with a broken heart. At least I had work and cleaning up the apartment back into a livable space to keep me preoccupied. But even with being busy, the time seemed impossibly long. And yet, my heart was still aching each time I thought of the sheriff and how his green eyes had stared helplessly at me. If he had asked me to stay, asked me just once, I would have stayed.

He didn't ask. Not once. He had demanded.

Nate had done the same thing that Jason would have done. He told me what I had to do without asking. It hadn't been about trying to protect me. What had happened with Nate was about control.

I would be damned in hell before I let any man have control over me ever again. I wasn't that woman anymore. I would never be that woman again.

Since that day, I hadn't heard from him once. He had skipped Saturday drinks with his sister, choosing to avoid me instead of carrying on a tradition I suspected was years old. He was a creature of routine, and him avoiding the bar spoke volumes. Even Kayleigh was starting to wonder where he had gone.

Now, I was sitting on my couch for the third weekend in a row, eating ice cream and watching movies. There was a storm raging outside. Thunder rolled every few minutes, and flashes of lightning lit up the sky. The metal staircase outside was making noise as the rain and wind pounded against it.

With a sigh, I got up and checked the door, making sure I had locked it before heading back to the couch and my tub of ice cream. I pulled the blanket over my legs, selecting another movie to watch.

As the wind howled, I heard a knock at the door. My heart was hammering in my chest as another knock soon followed, the dialogue of the movie I was watching fading into the background. A third followed. It had to be something hitting the door. Nobody would be coming over here, especially not this time of night. Something was knocking against the door. There had to be some sort of reasonable explanation for what was happening.

It's just the wind rattling the door, I thought as I leaned back deeper into the couch. *Only the wind. Nothing else is out there. My mind is just playing tricks on me because I stayed up too late.*

There was a bang against the door, too loud to be a knock. My heart was pounding in my chest as I reached for my phone. My hands were shaking as I dialed the only number I could think of. There was no time to think twice about whether calling him was the right move. I crossed my fingers, hoping that he would pick up.

"Lauren," Nate's deep voice said as soon as the call connected.

"Nate, I think someone is trying to get into my apartment."

"Listen to me carefully," he said without missing a beat. "I need you to stay quiet and get to a room with a lock on the door. Get in there and lock it until I get there."

In the background of the call, I could hear shuffling before the truck door slammed. I got up from the couch, grateful I had closed the curtains. There was another thud against the door as I crept to my room and shut the door.

It was getting harder to convince myself that it was my overactive imagination and staying up late to watch horror movies. That's all it could be out there. Nobody was trying to get in. I was irrational and looking for an excuse to get Nate over here.

But what if there is someone out there?

That wasn't a risk I was going to take.

"Nate," I said, twisting the lock. There was another large thump. "I'm scared. Please hurry."

"I'm on my way now, Lauren. I'm just down at the station, so I'll be there in a few minutes. Just lock the door until I get there. Stay on the phone with me. You don't have to say anything. Just stay on the line so I can hear that you're alright."

I twisted the lock and leaned back against the door, sliding until I sat down. On the other end of the line, I could hear Nate's steady breathing, even as my blood rushed to my head. The station was ten minutes away. All I had to do was stay locked in the room for another ten minutes, and Nate would be there. He would help me.

I wish there had been somebody to help me months ago, I thought, thinking about the night I finally left Jason.

Coming home early from a night out with my friend had been dumb luck. I shouldn't have been home early. However, I wouldn't have gotten the recording if I hadn't gone home until I was supposed to. That recording was the one thing I had needed to set myself free.

Seven weeks before I got the recording, I knew the marriage would end. When I looked in the mirror, I was so far from the person I used to be that I didn't recognize the woman staring back at me. The woman in that mirror had been a shell of a person. She was weak.

I had never been weak.

That day, I had walked out of the washroom after staring at the woman I didn't know for far too long. When I had joined Jason by the car, ready to go to an important dinner, he insisted that I had made us late.

That day was the first and last time he left a mark on me.

I took a deep breath, listening to Nate's breathing on the other end of the line. I counted his breaths, trying to calm myself down and forget what had forced me to this point.

"Okay, Lauren, I'm outside right now. There's nobody on the stairs. It's just me, okay? I'm climbing the stairs now."

"Okay. Okay."

"I'm outside your door now. Come let me in." Nate sighed. "There's nobody here, Lauren. It was just the wind. You're safe now. Come let me in."

I took a deep breath and got to my feet, unlocking my bedroom door and crossing the room to the front door. I hung up the call and twisted the lock, opening the door. Before I could say anything, Nate crossed the threshold and pulled me into a tight embrace. He buried his face in my neck, his arms tightening around my waist.

The embrace was unexpected, and I froze in his arms. He stepped back after a moment, his arms dropping to his sides. I felt the loss immediately. Being in his arms had made me feel safe. It was as if I was protected from the world around me. Nothing would have been able to hurt me as long as Nate was near and holding on.

Without his arms wrapped around me, I felt vulnerable and exposed.

At that moment, he was the one person keeping my head above water since I couldn't do it by myself anymore. I needed him by my side. I needed to know that one person in my life would protect me.

"Sorry," he said, his face turning red as he looked down at me. "I shouldn't have done that."

"That's all you have to say? After three weeks, you're sorry for hugging me?" I shook my head and ran a hand through my hair. "You can go now. I'm sorry for ruining your night."

"Lauren, don't start with that shit."

"I'm not starting with any shit. I told you that you could go now."

"Fuck, Lauren, I'm not going anywhere. Would you just stop running your mouth for five minutes and let me talk?"

I crossed my arms, cocking one hip and staring at him. "Fine."

"You're infuriating," he said, moments before closing the small gap between us.

His mouth pressed against mine as his fingers weaved their way through my hair, pulling me closer to him. Our bodies pressed together as he kicked the door shut behind him.

Nate's hands traveled down my body, his finger gripping my hips as I weaved my fingers into his hair. Our mouths slanted against each other, the kiss searching and desperate.

His mouth left mine, trailing down my neck, alternating between kissing and nipping at the skin. I moaned as his fingers slipped beneath my shirt, splaying against the skin there. Heat spread wherever he touched.

I ran my hands down his chest, stopping at the hem of his shirt. His hands left my waist long enough to pull his shirt over his head. Within seconds, his mouth was back on mine. My fingers trailed along his muscled torso, trying to commit him to memory.

"Bedroom?" he asked, his mouth leaving mine to trail down my neck again.

"Yes," I said.

He quickly picked me up, my legs wrapping around his waist as he carried me to the bedroom. Nate groaned as I ground myself against him, trying to relieve some of the tension building at my core.

Nate laid me down on the bed, kneeling between my legs. He looked down at me, his eyes warm as he surveyed my body.

"You are stunning," he said before reaching for my top. I helped him pull it off before taking off my pajama shorts and tossing them to the side.

For a moment, I wanted to cover up. He was the first person I had been naked in front of besides my husband in nearly a decade. Before I could even cover myself, his mouth wrapped around my nipple while his fingers found my clit.

I writhed against him as he nipped at my skin. Nate chuckled lowly, moving to the other breast and showing it the same attention he had shown the first.

"Fuck," he groaned, pressing his erection against me.

I reached between us, opening the button on his pants and trying to shove them off his hips. Nate raised his hips, helping me get his pants and boxers off before kicking them to the floor.

"Much better," I said, leaning forward to kiss his neck. Nate groaned, pressing himself against me again.

My hips bucked against him as he pressed against my clit harder. Nate trailed kisses along my body, nipping and sucking as he plunged two fingers into me. I came apart around him, writhing as he curled his fingers, drawing another orgasm out of me.

"Condom?" he asked.

"Nope. I'm on the pill."

"You're okay with this?"

"Shut up and fuck me already."

Nate chuckled and lined his cock with my core, hesitating for a moment before slowly thrusting. His moan filled the room as I hooked my legs around his waist, moving in time with him. We fell into a steady rhythm, my nails dragging down his back as he picked up speed, moving his hips faster.

I could feel my inner walls closing around him, squeezing him tighter and tighter until stars danced across my vision. I moaned, digging my nails into his back.

"Fuck, you feel good," he said, pulling back as he found his own release.

Nate fell to the bed beside me, rolling onto his side to look at me. I rolled onto my side, tucking an arm beneath my head. He smiled softly, his entire face lighting up in a way I hadn't seen before. His arm wrapped around my waist, pulling me closer before he kissed my temple.

"I'm going to go lock the door," he said, getting out of bed. I watched him walk out of the room, wondering what had just happened.

Why would he just leave like that? Didn't he want this as much as I did?

I thought that he wanted me. I thought that this might have been the beginning of the gap between us closing. Instead, it felt like someone had just rubbed salt into the open wound that was my heart.

There was a part of me that wanted more. That part wanted to run after him and demand answers. That part wanted to know why he was scared of everything we could be.

There was another part that told me to back off.

Maybe it was just sex. Maybe that's all I could let it be.

Emotions were running high, and I was damaged goods. I didn't have time for anything more than just sex, and I certainly didn't want to drag him down with me. No matter how safe he made me feel, we had both lost control.

When he returned, I pushed all the worried thoughts from my mind and enjoyed being wrapped in his embrace, no matter how temporary it might have been.

Chapter 7

Nate

The bed beside me was cold when I woke up and a hazy light filtered through the thin curtains. I sat up and looked around, but Lauren was nowhere to be found. I closed my eyes and opened them again, thinking that it might have been a dream and I would wake up back in my own house.

It was no use. When I opened my eyes again, I was still in her room. The sheets still smelled like the vanilla perfume she used and sex. I groaned and rubbed my face, propping myself up on my elbows and looking around.

"Lauren?"

There was no answer from any of the other rooms. I sighed and fell back into the pillows. She didn't seem like the type to run away the morning after, but I wouldn't put it past her either. Not after all that she had been dealing with these past few months.

I got out of bed and walked around the apartment, but she was long gone. Her shoes weren't by the door, and her keys were missing. My heart was beating quickly as I walked back to the bedroom and grabbed my jeans, tearing my phone out of my pocket. Disappointment flooded through me as I dialed her number.

"Hello, Sheriff," Lauren said when she answered my call.

"Hello, Lauren. Care to tell me where the hell you are so I can stop having a damn heart attack about what is going on right now?"

Every scenario possible was going through my mind. I still wasn't sure that it had only been wind at her door last night, but I wasn't going to tell her that and make her worry. There had been no sign of someone trying to break in, but her ex-husband was a cop. He knew how to cover his tracks if he was up to something.

All I could think of was her ex waiting for her outside the building and taking her when my back was turned.

"Stop being dramatic, Hollis. Everything is fine. I just needed some space."

"You know..." I said, my irritation growing along with the disappointment, "...most people would have woken up the person they were leaving in bed and told them that they were heading out."

"We aren't in a relationship," Lauren said, her tone sharp. She sighed. "Look, I need some space to think about this and what it means. This is new for me. So new. And big. I didn't think I would be with anyone else for a long time after my ex-husband; to be honest, it's scaring me. This was a big step. I need time and space. I will not get that space if I'm in that little apartment with you, trying not to sleep with you for the third time in twelve hours."

"Fourth," I said, smirking when I heard her irritated huff. "Get it right, Lauren."

"Remember the version of you that didn't want to talk to me? Can we go back to that for a few hours?"

"Or you could come back here, and we could talk about whatever is going through your mind like adults. I ruin a lot of things, Lauren. I'm not really interested in ruining this."

She hummed for a minute. I could hear the radio playing in the background. "Look, Nate, I really like you. A lot. And that scares me because up until last night, we hadn't talked to each other for three weeks, and the last time we talked, you were trying to tell me what to do. It reminded me of Jason, and I just can't deal with that."

"Lauren." My heart was sinking to my feet. The last thing I wanted to do was remind her of the man she had run from.

"Don't, please."

"Laur, are you really doing this right now? I thought that last night would have changed things for us. I thought we were finally going to get a chance to talk about whatever this weird thing between us was. And yet, here you are, running away from it. I'm not your ex-husband. I never meant to try to tell you what to do."

"But you did, Nate! You did," she whispered, her breathing hitching. "If you had just asked me to stay, I would have stayed. Instead, you demanded that I stay. You treated me like I'm yours to command."

"I didn't mean to."

"I know." She sighed. "I know."

"Then please come back so we can talk about this, okay? I really don't want this to be another one of those things I ruin."

"Nate, whatever feelings I have for you aren't enough right now, okay? I've got too much going on in my life, and you've got your own shit to deal with. And with Jason running around town the way he is, I don't want to put you at risk either."

"Lauren, I'm a cop. I don't need you to be worried about me. I'm more than capable of looking after myself."

"Nate, so is he." Lauren sniffled, and I immediately pictured tears rolling down her cheeks.

I sighed and ran a hand on my jaw, sitting down on her bed. "I'm not leaving until I know you're alright and we have worked this out. Your ex doesn't scare me. I think you're running scared because you don't know what to make of all this. Neither do I. That's why we should talk."

"Nate, just go home, okay? I'll talk to you when I'm ready."

"Fine."

I hung up and tossed the phone on the bed, falling back to stare at the ceiling. I could feel my chest tightening as I linked my hands behind my head. There was nothing I could do to change her mind, and there was clearly nothing I could say to get her back here. For once, ruining everything wasn't on me. She decided to walk away without figuring out what was happening between us.

For a moment, I was grateful for how the morning was going.

This was a mess, and I didn't know how to fix it. She was running from me, again, and I wasn't sure I wanted her to stop.

"Fuck," I groaned, getting up and pulling my clothes back on.

I liked her. I really liked her and had been suppressing that since we met. And yet, it might not be enough. It wasn't enough if she was right.

After gathering the rest of my things, I walked out of her apartment and closed the door behind me. I reached into the little potted plant beside her door, grabbing the key she had hidden inside. I locked the door before slipping the key into my pocket.

This wouldn't be the end of us if I had anything to say about it. I just needed to figure out how to fix it.

Instead of heading home, I walked into the station and headed straight for my office. I closed the door behind me before taking a seat at my desk and pulling up the search database.

"Jason Guthrie," I muttered, typing the name into the search bar. "Who are you?"

I should have researched about him before now. But it had been incredibly busy the last three weeks dealing with one issue or another in the town. Or maybe that's what I had told myself, trying not to think about Lauren and how much I had fucked that up.

But now, I really needed to find out all I could about her ex if I was going to protect her. I had no evidence that he was the one who had burgled her apartment, and the case had gone cold, the blue file mocking me in my open cases folder.

As records of his time at a police academy came up first—along with articles on awards he had won and cases he had been involved with—I scowled at the grin on his face, wondering what Lauren saw in a man like him in the first place.

Jason Guthrie was young but had worked his way through the ranks quickly. He had one recommendation from a superior after another, and not one of them had flagged how he was treating his wife.

Although maybe they had.

I knew what the city cops were like. They thought they were better than their peers and kept their noses turned up. They thought that their families were a reflection of themselves and kept them on a tight leash.

That was part of why I had chosen to be an officer in a small town instead of the city. I had more freedom to move along at my own pace. There was no pushing for higher ranks as soon as I got the next promotion. There was time for a life without posturing and pretending to be something you weren't.

Lauren had been the wife of a cop who thought appearances were everything. I could see how that would be a problem even after only knowing her for the past few months. She was a spitfire who spoke her mind and didn't give a damn about who she was talking to.

While her attitude pissed me off more often than not, it also kept the chemistry between us. She wouldn't just take whatever I was saying at face value. She challenged me.

Lauren was the kind of woman that made me want to be a better man.

Of course, I could see how much her personality would be a problem for a man trying to build his career. It would irritate a lesser man who only gave a shit about what was going on in his life.

She deserved better than that, and she deserved better than me.

I sighed and pushed back from my desk, running a hand down my face. After seeing how connected her ex-husband was, I wasn't surprised that she was worried. He could pull all kinds of strings without anyone knowing what he was up to.

"Fuck," I said, getting up from my desk and pacing back and

forth in front of the large window that overlooked the town square. My phone started ringing, Sarah's name flashing across the screen. I scowled and considered ignoring her call, but if I did that, she would only march down to the station and make the situation that much more miserable.

"Hello, Sarah."

"You're an idiot, you know that?" she said, her tone cutting deep.

"And why, may I ask?" I asked, even though I knew exactly what we were talking about.

"You know full well what I'm talking about. Why the hell are you letting Lauren just walk out of your life without a fight? You're making a huge mistake."

How did she know?

I had wanted to ask, but it wasn't a surprise to me that Sarah might be privy to what was going on between me and Lauren. Her, Lauren, and Kayleigh were becoming fast friends. At least Lauren had people she could confide in. I sighed, comforted by that.

"She made it perfectly clear that this is all too much for her," I said, sighing as I caught sight of the one person I wanted to see more than anyone else.

Lauren was sitting on one of the benches, her knees drawn to her chest. Kayleigh sat beside her; Bryce settled between them. I watched Lauren play with Bryce, a toy car in his hand, as he drove it up and down her legs. She tilted her head back, laughing as Bryce drove the car off her knee and flipped it through the air.

"Are you even listening to me?" Sarah asked, sounding breathless as if she had gone on a tirade again.

"Not really."

"You need to fix this, Nate. You've never been happier than when you were with her. I love you, and I want to see you happy. Fix this with her."

"I don't know what to do, Sarah."

"I don't know what you're going to do either, but you'll be the biggest idiot to have ever walked the earth if you don't fix this."

"Are you done calling me an idiot yet?" I asked, staring at Lauren through the window.

"Yes. I'll talk to you later."

"Love you, Sarah."

"Love you too, idiot."

After tucking my phone back in my pocket, I stepped back to the window and looked at Lauren. She was standing now, with Bryce in her arms, and spinning in quick circles. She looked as if she didn't have a care in the world.

I wanted to go outside and demand that she talk to me, but that would only put more distance between us. Instead, I closed the curtains and sat back down at my desk.

For now, I would have to sit back and let her have her space. If she wanted to continue whatever was happening between us, she would.

At least, I hoped she would.

Chapter 8

Lauren

I thought telling Nate I needed space and time to think wouldn't feel like ripping my heart from my chest, but it had. Every single day for the last month, it felt like I had ripped my heart out of my chest before starting to stomp all over it. Telling him I needed space was supposed to be easier than this. It wasn't supposed to hurt as much as it did.

The nights that hurt the most were Saturdays. Nate wouldn't show up for his normal drinks with his sister. Instead, he would arrive just as I was closing the bar and wait in his truck without saying a word as I locked the door. His truck would sit in the parking lot, illuminating the staircase to my apartment until I had locked the door and turned on the living room light. Seconds after that, the truck's engine would roar, and Nate would disappear from my life for another week.

I knew it was my fault, but it was surprisingly easy for him to avoid me in a small town. He seemed to have no problem staying hidden away until Saturday nights.

I wish that I could say the same. I spent more time out than ever, walking around town and trying to catch glimpses of him wherever I went.

Though my little adventures were great for meeting new people in Willow Town, they were less than stellar for easing the pain I had put onto my own heart. All those walks around town only made me wonder where he was hiding and who with. He was an attractive man who could find another woman easily.

Why am I even thinking about him finding another woman when I'm the one who pushed him away? I thought as I ran a hand through my hair and took a shaky breath.

Running away from him the morning after we slept together had been a bad idea, but it was the only thing I could think of doing. When I woke up that morning, a note had been sitting on my living room floor. I had picked it up with shaking hands, seeing Jason's familiar writing on the envelope.

Pictures were inside the envelope of me and Nate arguing or leaving the bar together. One picture was taken when he pulled me into a hug that night. In each picture, there were gouge marks where Nate's eyes should have been.

It was a clear warning, so I did what I had to do.

I broke my own heart to keep the man I loved safe.

With a sigh, I leaned back on my couch and closed my eyes, trying to erase the thoughts of the last month from my mind. There was nothing I could do about it now. I had made my choices, and I was stuck with them.

That didn't stop me from opening my eyes and grabbing my phone, scrolling through the contacts to his number. If I called him over now, would he even come?

Don't do it, I thought, tossing the phone across the couch, and reaching for the remote instead. I flipped through the movies, looking for something that would distract me for another night.

When I found nothing, I grabbed my phone again and gave in to the little voice that had been begging me to call him for the last month. I missed him more than I thought I would. I wanted him to come back so we could fix things. I wanted to apologize for what I had done. I wanted to beg him to let me back into his life.

"Lauren," Nate said, his voice deep and raspy. "You know, some people like to sleep when it's two in the morning."

"I thought you might not be one of those people," I said, my heart hammering in my chest. This was a bad idea. Even if I told him what was going on, there was no way he would ever forgive me.

"Lauren, I don't want to be rude."

"That's a pleasant change."

"Laur, stop," he said, sighing. "It's been a month, and now what? Now you want to talk?"

"I have a lot of explaining to do. Will you come over so I can do it?"

There was a long pause on the other end of the line. I could hear his steady breathing hitch before he exhaled.

"Fine, Laur. I'll be over there in twenty."

"Thank you."

"Don't thank me yet. Bye, Lauren."

"Bye, Nate."

After I ended the call, I tossed the phone to the side and pulled my thin blanket up to my chest. The cushions enveloped me as I put on a mindless movie and waited for Nate to arrive.

Barely five minutes after I put the movie on, there was a knock at my door. I frowned, grabbed my phone, and walked to the door. If Nate was coming from his house, it would take him the twenty minutes he had said.

I looked through the peephole, and my heart leaped to my throat. Jason stood on the other side of the door. I slowly backed away from the door, listening to Jason wiggle the handle. I heard a heavier thump against the door as I reached my bathroom.

My palms were sweating as I closed the door and turned the lock. Nate would be here soon. I just had to hope that my front door was enough to keep Jason outside until then. There was another thud against the front door.

"Lauren, let me in. You have been avoiding me for too long, and it's time we talk," Jason yelled, his voice carrying through my apartment and sending a shiver down my spine.

I fumbled with my phone, dialing Nate's number again. It went to voicemail. I sighed and slumped down against the bathroom door, sitting on the cold tile and feeling the tears start to drip down my cheeks. I wiped away the tears and shut my eyes, hoping Nate would drive a little faster.

At that moment, I was glad I had given the spare key to Kayleigh last week after Nate had handed it back instead of returning it to the flower pot.

"Lauren!" Nate's voice called through my apartment. "Laur, I'm here. Open up."

Shaking, I got to my feet, the steady thudding of the door for the last twenty minutes still playing through my mind. I crossed the living room as quickly as I could, pulling open the front door, and throwing myself into Nate's arms.

"Please take me away from here."

"I will," he murmured, holding me tight. "I'll take you somewhere safe."

***

Nate kept his arm around me as we walked inside his house, my bags in hand. As soon as his front door was shut and locked behind us, I turned to him and looped my arms around his neck.

"Lauren," he said, his arms circling my waist. "What are we doing?"

"I need a distraction. Please. Anything. We can talk later, but right now, I just need to feel something other than terrified that my ex is coming after me."

Nate gave me a sad smile and brushed a strand of hair behind my ear. "I don't want to take advantage of you. We have a lot to deal with."

"Not tonight," I said, standing on my toes and kissing his neck. "Please, just not tonight."

He groaned as I nipped at his neck, trailing kisses until I couldn't reach any higher. In one smooth motion, his arms looped beneath me, lifting me up before pressing my back against the nearest wall. His mouth was scorching hot as he sucked and kissed my neck, tearing my shirt off and tossing it to the side. I arched my back as he kissed the tops of my breasts, his hand sliding around my back. The moment my bra fell away, his mouth was on my nipple while his hand tweaked the other one.

I ground against him, heat building in my core as I ran my hands through his hair and wrapped my legs tighter around him. His hardened cock rubbed against me, drawing a groan out of Nate.

Nate's mouth moved to the other nipple as he pulled us away from the wall and walked down the hall to the bedroom. He quickly put me down and pulled off my shorts and panties. Nate grabbed my legs, hooking them over his shoulders before his tongue swirled around my clit. I bucked against him, gripping the sheets as he continued to swirl his tongue, fingers dipping inside me.

My inner walls tightened around him as he thrust his fingers in and out. With a few more strokes of his fingers, I convulsed around him. Nate grinned as he hovered over me, kissing me hard before flipping us over.

"Ride me, baby," he said, running a hand along my hip.

I moved over him, trying to swallow the self-conscious feeling that washed over me. Nate's eyelids were hooded as he watched me, his cock bobbing as he propped himself up on his elbows.

"You're beautiful," he said as I hovered over him, running my hands down his muscled torso. "I love all your curves." His hands trailed over my waist before softly massaging my belly pooch. "I don't think I'll ever get used to how sexy are."

Nate's hands moved lower before grabbing my hips with a smirk and pulling me down onto him. I moaned as he sank deep inside me. He guided me as I rocked back and forth, his fingers digging into my hips as he thrust upward.

"Just like that, baby," he said, one hand weaving into my hair and pulling gently. I arched my back, changing the angle until my inner walls convulsed around him.

He groaned, his own release coming hard and fast as I slumped against him. I rolled to the side, tucking myself against his body.

"I missed you," I said softly, the words hesitant as I looked up at Nate.

Nate's fingers drifted along my side. "I missed you too. We need to talk, though."

"I know," I said, draping an arm across his torso. I took a deep breath and closed my eyes. "I love you."

His hand paused on my side, his body stiffening beside me. "Excuse me?"

"That's what I've spent all this time thinking about. I love you."

His fingers started drifting up and down my side again. "I love you too. Even though it's crazy and we barely know each other. I fell for you the moment we met."

"Say it again. I need to hear you say it again."

He smiled and kissed my temple. "I love you too."

Chapter 9

Nate

Lauren had spent the last three weeks living in my apartment, her belongings cluttering up my space and her early morning singing driving me insane when all I wanted to do was sleep in.

This morning, it was some rendition of a song that I barely recognized. I groaned and rolled over, burying my face in my pillow until I heard the shower running. My dick twitched at the thought of her in my shower. Instead of suppressing my feelings, I got up and walked into the bathroom, stripping my clothing down along the way.

The steam fogged up the mirrors and the glass door, but I could still see the silhouette of the curves I traced my tongue around the night before. I stroked my hard cock as I opened the door, grinning at her little squeal as I stepped inside.

"Morning," Lauren said, a lazy smile on her face as she reached down, her hand replacing mine. My head fell back as I groaned, leaning back against the wall as she toyed with me.

"Morning," I groaned, grabbing her wrist and using it to pin her against the wall.

Lauren smirked, one leg hooking around my hip as she pulled me into her. She moaned as I lined up and slipped inside, the hot water pounding against my back. Lauren's nails raked down my back as I thrust inside her, pushing her body up against the wall and keeping one of her hands pinned against the wall.

"Faster," she said, digging her heel into my back and urging me deeper.

I moved faster, letting go of her hand to rub her clit. Lauren came apart around me, her legs shaking as she gripped my shoulders. Her inner walls squeezed me tight. I kept my grip on her as I thrust deeper and faster. I moaned as I finished, my fingers digging into her soft flesh.

"We should probably get cleaned up," Lauren breathed as I set her back down. She gave me a playful smile and looped her arms around my neck.

"We have other things we need to do today, and if you keep pressing yourself against me like that, we're not going to get them done," I said, frowning down at her.

"Fine," she said, reaching for the soap. "Be boring."

"I will."

I kissed her temple before helping her wash her hair.

We had a long talk a few weeks ago. Lauren had been holding back more than I had known about. We had been sitting on the couch when she pulled out the envelope, showing me the pictures of us. My blood had boiled when I saw the fear on her face. It was then that she had admitted the only reason she pushed me away was to protect me.

At first, it had pissed me off. I didn't need her to protect me. I was supposed to be protecting her. Instead, I had failed her when she needed me the most. When I put myself in her place, I realized that I would have done the same if I were her. She loved me and had done what she thought she needed to. I couldn't fault her for that, even if I was angry with her.

Since then, I had kept my eyes out for her ex, but so far, I hadn't seen Jason around town. The officers at my station were running different daily routes, staying unpredictable, but none of them had seen Jason Guthrie either. Even unannounced checks at the only motel in town didn't lead to anything. He came and went with ease, and that was the part that bothered me the most.

He was comfortable sticking to the shadows and knew how to avoid the officers looking for him. I believed that he was unhinged in some way, though. He wouldn't have come here looking for her if he wasn't. He wouldn't still be lurking around town and trying to break into her apartment.

"What's got you looking so worried?" Lauren asked as we got out of the shower. "You've got that *I'm a scary sheriff* look on your face again."

"I *am* a scary sheriff," I said, my tone teasing as I grabbed two towels and tossed her one of them. "I'm just thinking about your ex."

"While I'm naked," Lauren said, drying herself off. "That's weird. Can't say that it's a turn on."

I laughed and rolled my eyes, heading off to get dressed. Once we were both dressed, we walked to the truck and headed into town. Living with Lauren was an interesting experience. It had been a long time since I had lived with a woman. Candles were starting to appear all over my house, and we were flying through food like crazy. Of course, that was probably my fault. I only bought what I had when I still lived alone. I wasn't used to sharing my meals with someone else.

"Why did you seem so awful when I met you? People only had good things to say about you, but you were cranky as hell," Lauren said as we drove down the dirt road.

"I don't know. Her theory is that I'm stunted emotionally. My sister thinks it's because our dad died when I was young, and I had to be the man of the family before I was even a teenager."

"I'm sorry to hear that. Was it rough?"

"It wasn't a great time. My mom struggled a lot with addiction for a few years after that. She got cleaned up a few years ago, but it was too late, and the damage was already done. She passed away in her sleep one night. Organ failure."

Lauren reached over, taking my hand and lacing her fingers with mine. "Those people are right about you, you know. You are a good man."

"I try to be."

She sat beside me, listening as I told her about my childhood and the years of caring for Sarah and my mother. Her thumb stroked across the back of my hand as she inserted her own stories of growing up with a pair of loving parents. We traded stories back and forth, and the ease between us warmed my heart even more. I grabbed her hand and kissed her knuckles as she told me about her ideal dream house, describing it in such great detail that it merged with what I had been working on for the better part of this year.

"How about I take you somewhere else instead of grocery shopping?"

"I'm up for anything."

I grinned and turned the wheel in the opposite direction. It was nearly an hour's drive to where we were going, but I didn't mind. Lauren connected her phone to the stereo and played all her favorite songs, singing along as loud as she could. I laughed as she danced in her seat, pulling out as many crazy moves as she could think of. We pulled off the road and onto an empty plot of land.

"What is this place?" Lauren asked as she got out of the truck and started walking around.

"It's where I'm going to be building a new house. Construction starts next week."

"You're building it?" she asked, looking up at the tall trees surrounding the property.

"Why not? I built the first one. I was thinking I could rent that property out to one of the families in town. Move into a place a little bit bigger."

"Oh?" Lauren asked, looking over her shoulder at me and arching an eyebrow.

I looped my arms around her waist and pulled her close. "Yes. I was thinking a lot about my future a month or two ago. I saw this cute blonde woman and her friend playing with the friend's child, and it got me thinking."

"Did it?" Lauren asked, turning around to loop her arms over my shoulders. She smirked and ran her fingers on my jaw. "Thinking about what?"

"I want all that one day. I want it with you, so I thought I better start working on our dream home."

"Our dream home?"

"Our dream home," I said, nodding. "Only if you want it, though. If not, I'll just build the coolest house around, and you can visit whenever you'd like."

"I want that too. It already looks so much like what I was telling you earlier on." She turned to me, a sparkle in her eyes. "Funny how life works out."

She laughed as we walked around the small space already cleared, and I showed her where all the rooms would be. Lauren's laughter surrounded us as we danced in the kitchen and ran down the hallway. By the time we came to a stop, we were holding each other and swaying back and forth to music playing in the truck.

"How about we go back home, and I show you the plans that were drawn up? You can make whatever changes you'd like."

"Sounds perfect," she said, smiling as we let go of each other and walked back to the truck.

***

When we got back to my house less than ten minutes later, the front door was wide open, and the glass windowpanes on either side of the door were broken. Shattered glass lay across the porch, and a baseball bat was leaning against the wall.

"What the hell," Lauren whispered, getting out of the truck and slamming the door behind her.

"Laur, stay here, okay?" I got in front of her and took her face in my hands.

"Nate, I'm scared."

"I know, baby. Go back to my truck. Call the station and request backup. I'm going in."

Chapter 10

Lauren

"Like hell you're going in alone, Nate," I said, my hands clenching into fists at my sides as he opened the passenger side door and reached beneath the seat. "Jason's in there. It has to be him."

Nate pulled out a little black box and entered a code before pulling out a gun. He checked the magazine and clicked off the safety. My eyes widened as he kissed my forehead softly before stepping back.

"You can't do this, Nate. Not alone. I won't let you," I said, trying to hold back the tears starting to blur my vision. "Please don't do this."

"Lauren, I'm not going to sit here and argue with you about this. I need you to be safe. You need to get back in the damn truck and call the station."

"Nate," I said. "This is a bad idea. Please. Just wait with me until the officers get here to help. You don't need to go in there."

"I'm not going to let him continue terrorizing you. This ends now."

At that moment, I could only see Nate's lifeless body lying on the ground. I could see Jason above him, already trying to figure out how he would hide what he had done. He would get away with it, and nobody would ever know the truth about what happened to Nate.

I couldn't let it happen. I wasn't going to let it happen. Nate was not going to risk his life to save me from my ex-husband. I was the one Jason wanted. Me and the recordings. I wouldn't let Nate get himself into trouble to protect me.

"You're going to get hurt," I said, my vision going blurry as tears appeared in my eyes. "I don't want anything to happen to you. I can't deal with him hurting you. He won't hurt me. Let me go after him."

"I'm not going to get hurt," Nate said, his hand coming up to cup my face. He kissed me quickly. "I love you. Get in the truck and stay there until the other officers arrive. Please. I can't do my job if I'm worried about you too."

"Please don't do this."

"Get in the truck, lock the doors, and call the station," he said before walking away.

I stared after him for a moment as he walked up the front porch steps, his gun held in front of him. After taking a deep breath, I got back inside the truck and locked the doors. My hands were shaking as I dialed the number for the station.

"Willow Town Police."

"It's Lauren. Get to the sheriff's house as fast as possible," I said, my voice shaking. "There's been a break-in. We think that there's somebody still inside. Sheriff Hollis has gone in on his own."

"We're sending two units there as fast as possible, Lauren. Where are you right now?" the person on the other end of the call asked. I didn't recognize their voice, but I suspected it was one of the few officers I hadn't met yet.

"In the truck. The doors are locked."

"Good. Stay there. Help is on the way. I'm going to hang up now to take another call. If something happens, call the Sheriff's personal line. I'll reroute it through to one of the officer's cell phones."

"Thank you."

When the call ended, I was left alone in the truck. Nate's house was a nearly twenty-minute drive away from town. Twenty minutes was a long time to wait for something to happen. My heart was pounding in my chest, and I could hear my blood rushing in my ears. Nate was in there alone, and there was nothing I could do to help him. I couldn't go charging in there, it would only distract him, and I didn't have a weapon. I would be no help to him. The best I could do was sit in the car.

Unless there was evidence.

There was no car in the driveway, but Jason had to have driven up here. It was a long walk, and there was no way he would have had the energy to walk that far with how hot and humid the day was.

I got out of the truck and walked down the long driveway, looking for tire tracks that didn't match Nate's. Not even my car had been up here. Sure enough, I found tracks that had been hastily swept through. They looked like they were barely visible, but they were there.

After snapping a few pictures, I started following the tracks. We hadn't noticed a car on the way up here, so it wasn't parked down by the road. That had to leave it somewhere on the property unless Jason was long gone. Based on who he was as a person, I suspected he was waiting inside for the perfect moment to strike. He would take what he wanted without any regard for the consequences.

I was halfway around to the back of the house when I heard the gunshots, and my stomach dropped to my feet.

"Nate!"

I ran as fast as I could to the front of the house, my heart pounding. Shattered glass crunched beneath my feet as I took the porch steps two at a time and raced into the house. Another gunshot echoed through the hallway.

"Nate!"

"Lauren! Get out of here!"

I ignored him, desperate to find him, even as I heard glass shattering. Nate shouted and more glass shattered. In the distance,

I could hear sirens shrieking.

"Nate!"

"Lauren, get the hell out of here!"

There was another gunshot before a vase a few feet away from me broke, glass spraying everywhere. I felt pieces scrape against my face, drawing blood as I dropped to the floor.

Jason and Nate appeared at the end of the hall, grappling over the gun. Nate groaned as Jason drove his knee into Nate's torso. Nate was quick to recover, slamming his elbow into Jason and yanking away his gun at the same time.

"Lauren, I just want to talk," Jason said, blood in his teeth as he struggled with Nate. "This would have all been over real quick if you'd have done what I told you to do."

I stood in the corner, pressing myself as far back as possible. Nate glanced at me before gritting his teeth. He turned the safety on before throwing his gun at me. I swore and leaned forward to catch it, the metal fumbling in my hands. Clutching the gun to my chest, I stared at Nate with wide eyes. Terror kept me frozen in place.

"Run! Protect yourself!" he yelled before lunging forward and catching Jason around the waist. The two men fell to the ground, trading punches.

I took one look at the gun in my hands before my fight or flight response kicked in. Jason punched Nate hard, blood spraying onto the floor. I screamed, tears running down my face before I took off running.

The sirens outside were getting louder. I started running back to the truck, trying to yank open the door as Jason came charging out of the house, blood on his hands. My stomach lurched as I looked at him before abandoning my efforts to get in the truck.

I was faster than Jason. I always had been. We had run together all through high school and kept up with it once we had graduated. It used to drive him insane that I could outrun him.

I hope I still can, I thought as I took off down the driveway in the direction of the sirens. All I had to do was run faster than Jason until the other officers arrived.

"Get back here!" Jason shouted, his footsteps pounding against the ground as he followed me. "You bitch! You ruined my life!"

"You ruined it yourself, you corrupt piece of shit!" I yelled back, determined not to let Jason know how scared I was.

Jason laughed, the sound low and dangerous. "When I catch you, I'm going to make you wish that you had never taken that recording in the first place. You don't know what I'm capable of, Lauren, and I think it's about time I showed you."

Nate was shouting from somewhere behind us, but I couldn't look back. I had to keep running. I had to keep the gun away from Jason.

Suddenly, I collided with the ground, and a heavy weight settled on me. I kept a tight hold on the gun, knowing I would be dead when Jason got his hands on it. He flipped me over.

"You think you can blackmail me?" he asked, leaning forward. Blood from his broken nose dripped onto my face. "You think you can threaten to ruin my career, blackmail me, divorce me, and then just get away with it—"

I drove my knee upward, into his balls. His rant was cut off as he fell to the side, clutching himself.

There was no time to waste. I got back to my feet and started running again. Jason was still groaning behind me as I sprinted down the driveway.

"Get back here!" he shouted, his booming voice echoing through the forested area around the house.

Glancing over my shoulder, I saw that he was back on his feet, and Nate was close behind him. I only had to keep running for a little while longer. The police would be here soon, and then we would be okay. We would be safe.

We had to be safe.

I could hear his footsteps getting louder as he got closer to me again. As I pushed myself harder, my chest was heaving, the sirens louder and louder. Cars whipped up the driveway, dirt flying behind them. The first car stopped, the sirens cutting off as two officers climbed out of the car and started running toward me.

"Drop the gun!" one yelled, aiming her gun at me. "Put your hands in the air!"

I stopped running and threw the gun to the ground as the second officer ran forward to grab it.

Arms wrapped around my waist, and I was tackled to the ground, the air knocked out of my lungs. I gasped for air as a heavy weight pressed against the middle of my back. The weight was only there for a matter of seconds before it was lifted off me.

"Lauren, are you okay?" Nate asked, kneeling in front of me with blood pouring from his face and onto his shirt. "Laur, baby, are you okay?"

"I'm fine," I said, panic rising in my chest as Nate helped me get to my feet. "I'm fine."

His arms wrapped around me tightly, holding me close. "You're fine. You're going to be fine."

"We're going to be fine," I said, tears rolling down my cheeks as I pressed my face into his chest.

We held onto each other for a while before he pulled back slightly. "I need to take care of this," Nate said, stepping away from me. "Give me two minutes, okay?"

I nodded, swallowing hard and trying to hold off my tears. "Okay."

Nate kissed my forehead before walking over to Jason. He stood over the other man, listing his Miranda rights. I stole a glance at Jason, saw the vile scowl on his face, and my life flashed before my eyes. How had it come to this? At some point, Jason and I were so stupidly in love, even voted for the couple who would last the longest in high school on top of being Prom King and Queen. That seemed like ages ago. How wrong everyone had been.

But for all the heartache and pain Jason had put me through, I was glad it brought me to the one man I knew deep down would only love me and make me happy.

***

After hours of questioning, I was exhausted. The district attorney and several federal agents had rushed from Crawford City to Willow Town, but it was still a long drive. When they arrived, I was pulled into a little room and asked thousands of questions. While I answered every question they had, my mind was on Nate. He had been whisked away to the clinic to deal with his wounds before he would be questioned.

"Thank you," Agent Rossi said, holding her notepad by her side. "I appreciate the information you have been able to provide us on Jason Guthrie and the recording you have sent. We will be in contact in a few days to discuss the next steps with you, but I suspect he will go away for a very long time."

"Thank you," I said, a weight lifting from my shoulders. It was finally over. My nightmare was finally over. Someone else knew the truth, and they would make sure that Jason could never get to me again.

"Do you need a ride anywhere?"

"Can you take me to the clinic on Main Street?"

Agent Rossi nodded and led the way to her car. She didn't say anything as she drove through Willow Town, and I didn't bother trying to start a conversation. I stared out the window, looking at the people who were staring at the car. In a few hours, they would all know what had happened.

When we arrived at the clinic, one of the nurses took me to Nate's room. I closed the door behind me as he looked at me from the bed.

"Are you okay? I wanted to go to the station with you, but they wouldn't let me," Nate said, getting out of the bed and crossing the room to pull me into his embrace.

"I'm okay," I said, tears slipping down my cheeks. "I'm okay now. I promise."

"I was scared, Lauren. I still am. I don't know what comes next, and I don't know how to keep you safe."

"I can keep myself safe, and Jason will be going to jail," I said, leaning into his hug. Jason was out of my life for good. "I don't know what comes next either. I just know I want to be with you. I was scared for a long time that you would be like Jason. I was worried about getting involved with another cop. I thought that it would be like repeating history."

"And what do you think now?" Nate asked, pulling away slightly.

"I think that you're nothing like him, and I never really knew what it was like to feel loved until I met you."

Nate's fingers weaved through my hair as he pulled me to him for a kiss. He pressed his forehead against mine, our breath mixing as his arms tightened around me.

"You are the only person I've ever been able to see a real future with," Nate said, sounding as if there was a lump in his throat. "I thought I was going to lose you. I don't ever want to feel that way again."

"I don't think this will be easy. You and I have a lot of our own baggage to deal with, but I know I want to spend the rest of my life with you."

"Good," Nate said with a smile, kissing me quickly again. "I wasn't planning on letting you go again. I don't have a ring yet, but I'm going to get you one and do this right."

I leaned back to look at his wounds, running my fingers lightly down his face. "I don't need a ring right now. I have you. I love you."

"I love you too," he said, a smile stretching across his face. "But I'm going to buy you that ring someday."

"Someday is good enough for me."

"Stay with me?"

"Forever."

Epilogue

Nate

One year later

Lauren's hair was shining beneath the sun as she tilted back her head and laughed while our dog rolled around in the grass. We had gotten the dog a few months after moving into the house we built. Lauren thought all the big halls had been too empty and quiet. Her solution had been bringing home the dog one night and insisting that the golden retriever would be staying.

I had been powerless to refuse her like I was with most things these days. All it took was one little flash of that stunning smile, and I was a goner. She had me wrapped around her little finger, and she knew it.

It didn't bother me. She was wrapped around mine too.

"What are you thinking about?" she asked, twisting her engagement ring.

"I'm thinking about the wedding," I said, not bothering to tell her that she had me whipped. She already knew that.

"Oh?" she asked, a smile playing on her lips. "What about the wedding?"

"We should run away and elope tomorrow."

I didn't care when we got married. All I wanted was for Lauren to have the wedding of her dreams. As happy as I would have been to run away and elope, I knew that wasn't what she wanted.

"Sarah would kill me," Lauren said, grinning at the mention of my sister.

In the past year, the two had grown closer than ever. Add Kayleigh into the mix, and most Saturday nights, there was a trio of women gathered around my table drinking wine while Bryce raced his trucks through the house.

"Yes, she would."

"I guess we aren't eloping then," Lauren said, tucking her hands into her sweater pockets while a breeze blew harder, shaking the leaves in the trees.

"Guess not."

I took a sip of my coffee and stared at the line of trees surrounding the property. One day, I wanted to cut down more of the trees and build a pool and pool house. It would last us for years, and the kids we both wanted would love it growing up. We could be the house they brought their friends over to.

It was strange what a year and a half could do. Lauren had waltzed into my life and changed everything. She showed me that a life of isolation was nothing to be content with. She made me want the groups of friends over every week and the laughter that filled my kitchen. Lauren had been the one to change everything for me in a matter of months.

"You've got that look on your face again," Lauren said, smirking as she looked at me.

"What look?"

"The look you get when you're thinking about how much you love me."

I laughed and shook my head. "Maybe I was."

"I knew it." She sighed and twisted in her seat, draping her legs over the arm of her chair. "I love you too."

"I know," I said, sticking my tongue out at her.

Lauren laughed and shook her head, pulling her hand out of her pocket. She handed me a slim box wrapped in black paper. I raised an eyebrow as I looked at her. Lauren shrugged and nibbled on her bottom lip, sticking her hands back in her pockets.

"What is this?"

"Open it."

I set my coffee to the side and unwrapped the box. She stared at me as I lifted the lid, her eyes never leaving mine.

"What's this?" I asked, confused by the black and white picture I was looking at.

"Our baby."

It took me a moment to register what I was holding.

"You're kidding," I said, tossing the box to the side and getting up to pull her into a hug. "You're pregnant?"

"Two months today."

I grinned and held her tight, swinging her around in a circle. "That's amazing! Holy shit. We're going to be parents."

"We're going to be parents," she said, her grin spreading across her face as she laughed. "We're going to have a baby."

I laughed, kissing her, and wiping away the tears running down her cheeks. She hugged me tight, laughing and pressing her face into my chest. It seemed surreal, but it was happening. We were having a baby.

As I held her on the deck, I felt content for the first time in my life. Since Lauren entered my life, there were no more lonely nights. We were starting our own family, in a house we had built.

Life was good.

~ THE END ~

If you enjoyed *Mountain Man Sheriff,* take a look at a sneak peek of the next book in the series: *Mountain Man One Night Stand.*

Prologue

Naomi

I saw him from across the club as soon as he walked in. He didn't look like the other men surrounding me. There was something self-assured about how he carried himself that had heat rushing to my core immediately. His gray eyes scanned the room before he made his way to the bar.

"He's gorgeous," Leslie said, leaning closer to me with a mischievous smile. "You should go see if he wants to have a little fun."

My cheeks warmed as I rolled my eyes and kept swaying my hips to the beat of the music. Tonight was about forgetting the horrible afternoon I had had. Dropping Zach off at rehab never got any easier. My baby brother would always promise me that this would be the last trip, and then three months later, he would relapse.

I understood that he was struggling with addiction, but sometimes I wished I wasn't the only one fighting for his sobriety.

"You should go after him," Caroline said as she slithered her body along Leslie's, drawing the attention of a few different men in the club.

"I'm good here," I said.

There were more than a few reasons why a one night stand with a stranger was a bad idea. There was too much going on in my life. I didn't need to risk another potential complication.

We danced together; laughing and moving to the music until our drinks were empty and sweat coated the back of my neck. I held my empty beer bottle up to my friends before nodding to the bar. They grinned at me before moving back into the middle of the dance floor.

I weaved my way through the crowd to the bar. The bartender was leaning against the other end of the bar, talking to a small group of women. I sighed, knowing it would be a long wait, and climbed onto one of the empty stools.

"Hey," the man beside me said. I turned to look at him, shocked to be staring into his piercing gray eyes. "I saw you dancing out there. You're good."

"Thank you," I said, offering him a polite smile. "You should come dance with me."

"Dancing has never really been my thing. I'm better with my hands."

All thoughts of avoiding a one night stand flew from my mind. Seeing him from a distance had been completely different than seeing him up close. He was clean-shaven with a sharp jaw. Everything about him oozed confidence. He was the kind of man I would stay away from if I met him on the street.

Which was exactly why I started considering one night of fun with him.

The bartender came back over and stopped in front of me. "What will it be?"

I looked at the man beside me. "Shots?"

He grinned. "Tequila."

The bartender quickly poured the shots and set them in front of us. I downed the shot before setting the glass back on the bar. The man beside me drank his own before handing the bartender a bill.

"Keep the change," the man said.

"What do you say we get out of here?" I asked, crossing one leg over the other. The hem of my short black dress rose higher, and his gaze immediately dropped to my bare skin.

"One night? The hotel I'm staying at is close by."

"One night."

He got up and offered me his hand. I sent a quick message to my friends, letting them know where I was going before taking his hand. The man led me through the crowd and into a car already waiting by the curb.

A limo? Who is this man?

"What's your name?" he asked as the door closed behind us. "Eric, my hotel, please. And some privacy."

"Of course, sir," Eric, the driver, gave a quick nod before disappearing in front of the divider.

I smirked.

"My name...not important," I said, moving to straddle his lap.

His hands gripped my hips as his mouth met mine. I could feel his cock hardening beneath me. I pressed down against it, rubbing myself against him through his jeans and moaning at the sensation.

I should have probably waited until it was just the two of us, but I wasn't really thinking at the moment. I was trying to go with the flow.

Something I hadn't done in many years.

The man moaned as I tore my mouth from his to start kissing down his neck. His hands slipped below my dress, kneading my ass as he thrust upward. He pulled one hand away from my ass and removed his wallet, finding a condom within a second. Then, he pulled back long enough to reach between us and unzip his jeans, raising his hips high enough to shimmy his clothing down.

I lifted my dress higher as he rolled the condom on. His fingers slipped between my legs, stroking against my clit slowly. I writhed against him, not wanting to wait any longer.

His hand knotted in my hair, tilting my head back as I lowered myself onto his cock. He groaned, kissing the tops of my breasts as I rode him. I could feel the release building, but he quickly flipped us over, pressing my back against the seat.

He kissed down my body, pushing the dress higher. His mouth found my clit, his tongue circling the bundle of nerves until I was bucking against his face. I moaned as his fingers entered me, thrusting deep and fast until my inner walls were clenching around him.

"Come for me," he said, his voice rough.

He continued to work his tongue over my clit as I came, stars dancing across my vision. Before I could catch a breath, he thrusted his cock deep inside me, and I was chasing another release.

The limo came to a stop as he finished. We were quick to rearrange our clothing before getting out. I avoided looking at Eric, knowing we weren't exactly silent back there. Thank God the gray-eyed man led me through the hotel, quickly. My heart thumped with excitement.

Our clothing only stayed on long enough for us to get into the hotel room. We fell into bed together, losing ourselves in each other's bodies.

What happens when Naomi gets the assignment of a lifetime, the break that she's been looking for? Will a secret bring her together with her one night stand, or tear them apart?

Book 2 is now available!

Printed in Great Britain
by Amazon

19366799R00058